RAISING THE
PERFECT CHILD

THROUGH GUILT
AND
MANIPULATION

You can do it!

Best wishes on your perfect child.

Love,
Virginia & Warren

RAISING THE PERFECT CHILD

THROUGH GUILT AND MANIPULATION

ELIZABETH BECKWITH

WILLIAM MORROW
An Imprint of HarperCollinsPublishers

RAISING THE PERFECT CHILD THROUGH GUILT AND MANIPULATION. Copyright © 2009 by Elizabeth Beckwith. All rights reserved. Printed in the United States of America. No part of this book may be used or reproduced in any manner whatsoever without written permission except in the case of brief quotations embodied in critical articles and reviews. For information, address HarperCollins Publishers, 10 East 53rd Street, New York, NY 10022.

HarperCollins books may be purchased for educational, business, or sales promotional use. For information, please write: Special Markets Department, HarperCollins Publishers, 10 East 53rd Street, New York, NY 10022.

FIRST EDITION

Designed by Ashley Halsey

Library of Congress Cataloging-in-Publication Data

Beckwith, Elizabeth.
   Raising the perfect child through guilt and manipulation/Elizabeth Beckwith.—1st ed.
      p.   cm.
   ISBN 978-0-06-175957-4
   1. Parenting—Humor. I. Title.
PN6231.P2B43 2009
818'.607—dc22

2009012959

13   OV/RRD   10 9 8 7 6

To my parents, Liz and Pat Beckwith,
the best (and funniest) mother and father
any kid could ever wish for.

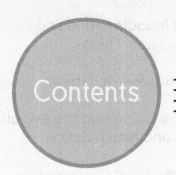

Contents

Introduction

When I was getting ready to have my first child, I read a lot of articles and books about babies and parenthood. One particular question kept popping up, and it scared the crap out of me—"What is your parenting philosophy?" What?! Parenting philosophy? Is this something I could register for at Baby-Style? As it turns out, before the baby even pops out, you're supposed to have a well-formed set of parenting principles to guide you. Sweet Jesus, help me! I could feel the panic setting in. The baby must have felt it, too, because it started kicking like crazy as if to say, "Bitch better get it together! Don't you know I need boundaries and shit?!" I don't know why my unborn child spoke like a street thug, but in my paranoid mind anything was possible if I didn't hurry up and get a philosophy going.

I took a deep breath and reflected on my own upbringing. Did my parents have a philosophy? After all, they were my parenting heroes. They raised four well-educated, well-adjusted, kindhearted kids, and they did it all without what appeared to be any sort of formal discipline. My head was spinning! Thinking back, I don't ever remember being "punished" for anything. I was generally a pretty good kid, but when I did do something bad, the only thing I remember was being filled with so much shame and guilt that any further punishment would have been child abuse. My parents must have known this. Come to think of it, they were always giving us lots of hugs and encouragement and making us feel like we were part of a team. That must have been why I felt so shitty when I did something that went against the unspoken team rules. But how did I know these rules if they were unspoken? Wait a minute, wait just a minute. It was because my parents openly talked disparagingly about people who did bad things, thereby reinforcing in my little mind that I never wanted to be like "those people" that my parents were so clearly disgusted by. There were no abstract lectures about how it is "wrong to steal." Instead, there would be a lively dinner conversation about the bastard employee/relative who stole from the register at my parents' candy store.* My father would animatedly hold court: "What kind of sick son of a bitch steals from his own family?!" My young mind carefully processed the information: *I will never steal from anyone, but especially not from family.* My parents are geniuses! I will adopt the unintentional philosophy of my own parents and *that* will be my parenting philosophy. I thought to myself, *If my parents wrote a book about parenting, it would be called* How to Raise the Perfect Child Through Guilt and Manipulation.

Since my parents had no interest in deconstructing what came naturally to them and reproducing it for the masses, I decided to attempt it myself. What follows is my twisted take on a traditional parenting guide.

One minor note: Although I have changed the names of

---

* I realize there are like nine different people who probably think that I'm talking about them right now. Relax, it's not you. I promise.

many of the people mentioned in the personal essays, I didn't change the names of the people closest to me. Because of this, you may notice a lot of different characters who possess the same name. My mother and I are both named Elizabeth. A cousin *and* a brother named Jimmy. A dad named Pat, a husband named Pat, and a brother named Patrick (to say nothing of the Aunt Pat and cousin Patricia who are *not* mentioned). This is partially a coincidence and partially a side effect of coming from a traditional Italian family where everyone is named after somebody. Either way, it's real. I believe the names are spread out enough not to cause confusion, but I thought I should mention it, lest you think you are losing your mind.

Elizabeth Beckwith

RAISING THE
PERFECT CHILD

THROUGH GUILT
AND
MANIPULATION

1

Creating a Team:
"Us Vs. Them"

A family should be a team. A tribe. A group of people living together who, though all individuals, share a common set of values and principles. It boils down to this golden rule: "We do things a certain way, and everyone else is an asshole." This is the foundation of the Guilt and Manipulation philosophy. Without establishing this precedent, none of the other steps will be effective. Now, is this something you should put on a bumper sticker and slap on your minivan? Of course not; that would be trashy. Like many of the lessons you will learn in this book, this is something that goes unspoken. It's tricky business, but before long, relaying to your children who the jerks are via telepathic messages will be second nature.

Before we go any further, let me give you a list of assholes to familiarize yourself with. Every family is unique, so your list may be a little different than mine—although if your list is too different, the possibility exists that you are an asshole yourself and need to take a good, hard look in the mirror before you reproduce again.

Assholes

- Parents who "party" with their kids.
- Sloppy, drunk people. Look, I'm not going to pretend that I've never been publicly intoxicated and embarrassing. I'm sure most of you have been this person at various moments in your lives. But it is important to openly disapprove of this in front of your child with comments like, "How embarrassing!" or "What a fool!" It is also important to make a pledge not to be that person ever again. You have kids now. You don't want to be the Dressed Inappropriately for Your Age Loser puking in the parking lot of a bar full of college students.
- People who steal.
- People who drive trucks that have been lifted by some hydraulic system. They usually have giant tractorlike tires and some kind of offensive bumper sticker along the lines of *I Don't Give a F#@k!*
- Conversely, people who drive tiny, lowered cars. You know the ones. They've turned their Honda Civic into a racecar with tacky purple lighting. They almost murder you on the freeway as they re-create scenes from *2 Fast 2 Furious.*
- People who speed down residential streets and/or in parking lots.
- Couples who display overtly sexual affection in public. Especially teenagers. I am looking at two of them right now as I type this, and I am about to throw up. One of them has a Mohawk. Double whammy.
- People who cut in line. It's not okay when you're five,

and it's not okay when you're fifty-five. Wait your effing turn!

This is just a partial list, but hopefully it will prove helpful to you.

Recognizing an asshole is one thing; indoctrinating your children to find the same people offensive is another. It is important to begin the brainwashing early, while they still worship you. It has been proven that children are more adept at learning foreign languages when they are very young; the same is true of learning to identify an asshole. Now, before I go any further, let me make something clear. This is not about being rude to every person who falls into this category. Not at all. In fact, your child will often witness you being kind and generous to some of these jerks. You may even swim in the same genetic pool as some of these people. This is about one thing: *not letting your child grow up to be an asshole.* How? Three steps.

1. Give your child tons of support, hugs, and encouragement from an early age, establishing the positive support system of your team.
2. Speak loudly and disparagingly of people who do bad things. For example, "Can you believe how fast that guy is driving through the parking lot? What a moron! That's how people die!" (It's always good to sprinkle the fear of death into these lessons whenever possible.)
3. More hugs and encouragement, reinforcing the notion of "Thank God we're not like *those* people" and "Let's

just try to stay the hell away from people like that so they don't kill us."

Step 1 should come easily enough. What parent doesn't have a natural inclination to hug and encourage his or her child (other than the terrible parents, of course)?

Step 2 is a little trickier. This is where you really have to hone your skill of *brainwashing without being obvious*. The key here is to really believe what you say and to learn to stop editing yourself so much. New parents usually get into the habit of being very careful with what they say in front of their child. To a certain extent this is good. You don't want to freely drop the F-bomb in front of your two-year-old and have her toddling around the supermarket chanting "muda-fuka!" at the top of her lungs. But it is perfectly acceptable to say things like, "How disgusting!" or "What pigs!" when you see someone throwing a fast-food bag out their car window or a pair of thirteen-year-olds making out at the park. You want to get the point across regarding how you feel about the offending person using the strongest language possible short of profanity. This comes very naturally for me, but it may not come naturally for you. If you need a little assistance in this department, here is a list of phrases to help jump-start you. Even if you don't need help in this area, it is important to study this list, as other important lessons are woven within.

Helpful Phrases
- "Does she look like a hooker or what?"
- "How many Quaaludes did this guy take today?" You

may find a drug reference startling and think I am crossing a line, but actually this provides a nice segue into a conversation about drugs with your child. "Mom, what's a Quaalude?" "A drug, honey. It puts people in a trance. Look at this guy! He's walking around in la-la land, and meanwhile he's about to get hit by a car! I feel sorry for him; he probably lives in a Dumpster somewhere. I mean, look at him, when's the last time you think he showered?" What does your child take away from this? *I don't want to live in a Dumpster. I will never do Quaaludes. I love my mommy.* I realize Quaaludes haven't really been a threat to our nation's children since, like, 1978, but it's a funnier word than *heroin*. Plus, it was a real reference that my mother used with me as a child, so I have a soft spot for it. I'll never forget it. We were looking for a parking spot and this woman was zigzagging through the lot, pushing her cart, her head in the clouds. Without missing a beat, my mom yelled out, "Pop another Quaalude!"

- "What kind of a sick bastard steals from his own family? You've gotta be a real sick son of a bitch!" Yes, *son of a bitch* falls into the profanity category, but if used sparingly it can be a very effective phrase. Use at your own discretion.

- "You've gotta be a real lowlife to leave your three kids just 'cause you've got the hots for some floozy from work!"

- "You believe this guy? I just said 'Excuse me' to him and he doesn't even acknowledge me. He's either deaf or a shithead. Either way, he needs our prayers." Again, *shithead* should be used at your own discretion. I believe it is acceptable for age twelve and over, especially if paired with the concept of prayer, but use according to your own comfort level.

- "Look at Mrs. Johnson. She used to be so beautiful; now she looks like a raisin. That's what smoking does to you." It should be noted that neither my three siblings nor I smoke. I used to tell my mom that I wanted to smoke when I grew up. She would say, "Fine, when you're eighteen, if you want to smoke, you can smoke." Meanwhile, she made comments like the one regarding Mrs. Johnson all the time. Every time a newscaster with lines around her lips came on the screen, my mom would casually remark, "Must be a smoker; you can tell by all those lines around her lips." *I don't want lines around my lips! I don't want to look like a raisin!* Are you starting to see the beauty of this system?

As you may have noticed, what makes this so effective is the appearance of freedom. It is what is left unspoken, the seeds of suggestion, that are doing the work for you: *Sure, you can smoke if you want to; I think smokers lose their looks young, but hey, to each her own, sweetie.* There is no need for formal "sit-down" conversations about the difference between right and wrong. These lessons can all be gleaned by your child just from hanging out with you. How much more effective is a lively dinner conversation about your crackhead cousin who stole your car for drug money than a stilted, abstract "Well, son, stealing is wrong because . . ." chat? Think about it. I realize not everyone has the luxury of a crackhead cousin, but I'm sure you will find moments from your arsenal of family, friends, and work colleagues that can be exploited to strengthen your child's moral compass.

Let us examine more closely how effective this form of manipulation can be by examining my own upbringing. In the following essay you will see firsthand how my mother's words profoundly affected my attitudes toward sexuality. Pay close attention to the connection—you must focus; the burden is on you. Discussion questions will follow.

UP CLOSE AND PERSONAL
Crazy Girls, Hookers, and Me

"Does she really think she looks good in that? Who does she think she is, Barbarella?" Spoken in her barely faded Brooklyn accent, this was a typical comment from my mom while driving home from the mall on a Saturday afternoon. This was usually followed by a mini speech about how much sexier it is to be a mystery (with one or two remarks about how men don't like "girls with no asses" thrown in for good measure). There seemed to be an endless stream of inappropriately dressed ladies available for my mother's commentary. This may have been because we lived in Las Vegas, and a lot of those women were hookers. Although my mother would usually single out the actual hookers by saying something like, "Is that a hooker or what? I mean, hello!"

My mother's comments were not in vain. From the time I was four or five, I understood very clearly that it was much sexier to leave something to the imagination than to let it all hang out like a floozy. I've been told this is a matter of opinion, but if you like girls who look like whores then I will probably find a reason not to like you. Sorry.

This is not to say that we didn't have a lot of these types of women in our lives. We did. This was why it was so important for my mom to start early with the brainwashing. My cousin, a pimp at the time, would occasionally pop in for Sunday dinner with a scantily clad girl or two. Judgmental as my family is, we are incredibly warm and inviting, especially my parents. And when it comes to family (or even friends of family), everyone is welcome and no one leaves hungry. Over the years this has included pimps, whores, and the occasional post-op transsexual.

Having a pimp for a cousin is unusual, even in Vegas. I knew more people with a Pip for a cousin (as in Gladys Knight and the Pips) than a pimp.

"My cousin is a Pip."

"My cousin is a pimp too!"

"No, a *Pip*!"

"Oh! That's not the same thing at all. Although my cousin does wear a pastel suit and follows a black lady around!"

As a small child, I did not have any concept of what my cousin did for a living. All I knew was that he wore platform shoes and big purple hats and brought half-naked women to our house. Perhaps it should have been obvious, even to a four-year-old. Anyway, lest I think that wearing a large-looped crochet sweater with nothing underneath was normal, my mother would make a nearly audible facial expression or a biting comment after they left, to let us know that exposed nipples was not a fashion option. I had three older brothers, so unless they turned out to be flamboyantly gay Puerto

Ricans, they were not likely to make those choices anyway.*
The comments were mostly for my benefit, though she was
also broadcasting a not-so-subtle message to my brothers
about what would be an acceptable mate. "Acceptable mates"
were probably the furthest thing from their minds as they ate
their meatballs, pretending not to notice the Pocahontas sex
fantasy sitting across from them.

It wasn't just my cousin's employees. My beloved Aunt
Doris, my dad's sister, showed up at her son's confirmation in
a miniskirt and fishnets. Everyone loved my aunt dearly, so
she was spared my mother's comments. She was like a busty,
blond angel in go-go boots. Years later, Aunt Doris became a
born-again Christian and tried to tone down her look some-
what. At her baptism she wore an innocent, all-white dress.
Although when I look back at the photos of her rising from
the water and achieving salvation, I am struck by how much
it resembles a wet T-shirt contest, God bless her.

Raising children in Las Vegas presented a unique set of
parenting challenges, not the least of which was the ever-
present, oversexualized, female-exploitation subculture that
loomed over your children. Nowadays the entire country is
oversexualized as young girls willingly exploit themselves for
their fifteen minutes of fame. But when I was growing up, Las
Vegas was ahead of its time in this department.

I remember riding in the car on the way to second grade
at St. Viator, staring at the racy advertisements that were
plastered on the taxis that passed us by. I was particularly

---

* This image is not meant as a homophobic or racist stereotype. It is
based on one such character that I saw roller-skating through Washing-
ton Square Park while feeding pigeons with my Grandma in 1982.

obsessed with the one for a show called Crazy Girls! I thought to myself, "They must be crazy, they're not wearing any pants!" as the tanned asses of eight showgirls stared back at me.

Although all of these influences didn't appear to affect my good-girl, follow-the-rules, obsessive-compulsive self, secretly they were on my mind. I would never dream of actually becoming like these women myself, but what was the harm in pretending that my Barbies were Crazy Girls!? Pretty soon all of my Barbies were jumping into their hot-pink Jeep and heading out for a wild night at the strip club.

By the time I was in seventh grade, my Barbie Dream House had transformed into a virtual Mustang Ranch. Malibu Barbie pranced around wearing not much more than her painted-on tan lines. The previously harmless Ken was suddenly donning Barbie's fur coat and bossing everybody around, saying things like, "Bitch better have my money!" Teenaged Skipper cried all the time and smoked a lot of dope to numb the pain of lost innocence and the rough life of the sex trade. I was really into my dark Barbie world, and my heart broke for these girls as though they had made these choices themselves and I had nothing to do with it. Meanwhile, I went on with my self-righteous little life, saying my prayers and studying for my exams.

There is a certain innocence in still having affection for Barbie when you're already twelve years old, even if your Barbies are drug-addicted hookers and Ken is a pimp with a God complex. At least *I* wasn't doing any of those terrible things, and I had no plans to ever do drugs or have premarital sex. And as far as I knew, no one in my class had those plans either.

Then I got to high school.

Oh my God, people were having sex and doing drugs! Those things were supposed to be reserved for our relatives that we spoke poorly of, not for friends of mine! Now when I drove to school there was an entire billboard for Crazy Girls! The naked asses appeared to mock me as I defensively bundled myself up in my oversized New York Mets starter jacket.

By senior year, the hedonistic activities of my classmates were no longer shocking, just kind of depressing. It's not easy being a virginal teenaged girl when your boyfriend and all his buddies have already visited a Chicken Ranch.* How was I supposed to compete with an enclave of exotic hookers from around the world? I pictured my short, skinny, seventeen-year-old boyfriend surrounded by a harem of nude women feeding him grapes as they shook their asses over his face. A similar scene had taken place years before on the third floor of Barbie's townhouse.

I survived adolescence in Las Vegas with my virtues only slightly damaged. I had some falls from grace here and there, but all in all I was one of the good girls. Even during my least dignified moments, I was never wearing an outfit worthy of my mother's comments (pretty much my only goal most of my life). I may have been doing things I would later regret, but I was probably doing them in a blazer and Doc Martens.

Not too long ago I was watching a documentary about Las Vegas showgirls. Perhaps *documentary* is not the right description for a show on E!, but you get the idea. They got to a segment devoted to Crazy Girls!, and I was hooked. Suddenly a

---

* *n.* whorehouse.

girl popped onscreen who looked familiar to me. Holy shit, I went to high school with her! I didn't know her very well, but she dated one of my boyfriend's good friends back in the day. While we were in high school she had won Miss Teen Nevada. This fascinated me as a kid because, although she was popular and attractive, she struck me as more of a plain Jane than the Cindy Crawford types I imagined taking the crown in a cutthroat beauty competition. I always just assumed that she must be some kind of classical piano prodigy who wowed them in the talent portion, or her dad "knew a guy."

Looking back, she was probably one of those girls with a "perfectly acceptable" face but a smoking-hot body. If someone's face didn't make me look twice, I was totally oblivious to her physique. It wasn't until I was twenty years old that I learned the power that the girls with the hot bods possessed.*

So there I was, enjoying my guilty pleasure of a lowbrow documentary when Miss Teen Nevada turned Crazy Girl comes on. And, yes, she had a smoking-hot body. Here she was, baring it all on stage. I'm sure the pageant panel would be proud, as would the administration of Bishop Gorman High School. Miss Teen Nevada had traded in her sash and crown for a G-string and nipple decals.

You would think that would be as "full circle" as I would come in my psychological relationship with Crazy Girls! It wasn't.

I had been living in Los Angeles for a few years when I booked a gig performing stand-up comedy at the Riviera

---

* If you would like to learn more about this enlightenment, please purchase my forthcoming book, *Elizabeth Learns That Tits Trump a Pretty Face.*

Hotel in Las Vegas. The Riviera is one of the few remaining "old Vegas" casinos, and it is the home to none other than Crazy Girls! The comedy club was actually right next door to the Crazy Girls! Theater. I couldn't believe my luck! In between the 7:00 and 10:00 shows, I would pop my head in and sneak a peek at the Crazy Girls. I don't know exactly what I was expecting. I never really imagined anything beyond the lineup of asses. "Oh, what surprises must be in store for me!" I felt like Charlie clutching the last Golden Ticket into Wonka's factory as I pushed open the door. What greeted me was not sleazy, and Gene Wilder in a velvet suit was nowhere to be found (at least not to my knowledge). Oddly enough, the show seemed kind of innocent. Compared to the slutty-looking women who currently grace the billboards of Vegas (overly made-up, nude blondes riding exotic animals, a look of ecstasy on their face), these topless, ass-baring ladies almost seemed quaint in their cute wigs and red lighting.

I felt an instant connection with these women, and it shocked me. I wanted to jump on the stage, hug them, and yell, "I feel you, my sisters, I feel you!" When I did stand-up comedy, I felt more naked and crazier than the Crazy Girls as I bared my soul night after night to an audience full of drunken morons who didn't appreciate me. People don't come to Las Vegas to see neurotic girls tell jokes. At least when someone yelled "Show us your tits" to a Crazy Girl, his wish would be granted. Maybe you gals aren't so crazy after all.

My mother came to every one of my fourteen shows that week. Afterward, we would usually stop for a bite to eat. Walking through an old casino like the Riviera is not like walking through the Palms. There are a lot of people playing the slots who are also hooked up to breathing machines. It has become increasingly difficult to tell the difference between prostitutes and college girls on spring break, but at the Riviera it is a little easier since most of the hookers are hooked up to breathing machines, too.

Occasionally, one of these women of the night would walk by us. Without saying a word, my mother would make one of her faces that spoke volumes. In my head I could hear the accompanying narration: "Is that a hooker or what?"

Yes, Mom. Yes it is. The bigger question is, did she have dinner at our house in 1979?

Discussion Questions

1. How is it possible to reconcile the fact that Elizabeth's Barbies were hookers with the idea that her mother's brainwashing was a success?
2. How can you, the reader, use your lowlife relatives as teaching tools for your offspring?
3. What facial expressions best convey disapproval?

> ### Homework!
> Practice the art of the "disapproving look" for twenty minutes a day. Depending on facial structure and ethnic background this will vary greatly from person to person. You'll know it when you see it!

Wow, I've barely finished typing and already I am being bombarded with reader mail. Let me take a moment to read and respond to a few:

Dear Elizabeth,

I am appalled! How can you imply that you are a good example of this philosophy's success when all of your Barbies were "drug-addicted hookers" and you dated a boy who visited a whorehouse as a minor? My book club just got into the biggest fight about this while going over the discussion questions. I am ready to light your book on fire and throw it in my former best friend's face!

Signed,
Shocked in Chamburg

Dear Shocked,
First of all, thank you for buying my book and including it in your book club. This is especially exciting to me since I have not even finished writing it. I apologize that I upset you, but I think you are missing the point. *My Barbies were hookers, NOT ME!* I used my imagination to channel all of those dark thoughts into inanimate objects. That is a parenting success on two levels:

1. I developed a great imagination.
2. I never looked like a whore.

What more could one ask for in a daughter?

Sincerely,
Elizabeth Beckwith

Dear Elizabeth,
I'm confused. What does your obsession with a show like
Crazy Girls! and your discovery that men like "hot bods"
have to do with parenting?

Yours truly,
Karen M.

Karen,
Very little. Sorry.

EB

Dear Elizabeth,
I think I am on the right track with my daughters, but how
can I influence all of the lost young women of America who
seem all too willing to "let it all hang out like a floozy"?

Sincerely,
Concerned

Dear Concerned,
I hear you. You are already doing a lot. Just by raising
your daughters well, you are impacting the world in a
positive way. I don't really believe in interfering with
other people's parenting, so in a lot of ways your hands
are tied. What you can do is write an "open letter"
to these young women expressing your concerns and
attempt to get it published in your local paper. I will
include an example on the following pages to give you
an idea of what I mean.

Sincerely,
Elizabeth Beckwith

Girls, Please Stop "Going Wild": An Open Letter to the Young Women of America

Dearest Young Women of America,

It has come to my attention over the past several years that many of you enjoy "going wild." By this I refer to the countless videos of "hot co-eds" flashing their breasts that are offered to me every time I sit down for an evening of Comedy Central. Apparently people who enjoy reruns of *Chappelle's Show* also enjoy the hilarity of girls in G-strings licking each other's nipples.

Upon first viewing of these advertisements, I must admit that my heart broke. I thought to myself, "Look at these poor, young lesbians. Unable to express their love for each other publicly, they are forced to hide out in what appears to be a low-budget production trailer and do their topless French kissing in there. God forbid they should be allowed to fondle each other out in the open on their college campus! Oh no, some meathead frat guy would probably gay-bash at the first sight of two naked girls rubbing their asses together while seductively eating ice cream cones. Oh, the gross intolerance!"

Then it was explained to me by a good friend that these weren't real lesbians at all, but young heterosexual girls attempting to titillate men through their girl-on-girl lovemaking. I was shocked. Oh, what a tangled web we weave, ladies!

It is easy to blame others: the media, the culture, poor role models. But as you stand on a speedboat, four Jell-O shots in, holding a can of whipped cream over your best friend's genitals, you may want to take a good, hard look into the slightly reflective bottom of that can and ask the topless girl staring back some tough questions.

For starters, "How badly do I want that *Girls Gone Wild* T-shirt?" I realize this is a badge of honor in some circles—the sorority girl equivalent of the Girl Scout cookie badge. But the reality is, and I hate to be the one to break it to you, you're about to shoot a porno—*and all you got was a lousy T-shirt!* At least real porno actresses get cash and cocaine.

Second, "What would my parents think?" For some of you, this may be a bit of a loaded question. Your father may have a collection of these sorts of DVDs stashed away in the basement rec room. Imagine when Daddy gets his latest video in the mail. Oh, to be a fly on the wall as he locks himself in the basement, deftly removing his pants, only to be greeted by the image of YOU, clad only in Mardi Gras beads, jokingly making your tits swirl around like airplane propellers. I think you will both learn a valuable lesson that day.

Lastly, "Can I ever imagine regretting this someday?" If you quickly answer, "No," then I can only imagine that your goals in life do not reach far beyond that of "professional escort" or "political scandal participant" (or some combination of the two). Please think hard about this one.

Pardon me for a moment as I turn into my mother, but what ever happened to *mystery*?

(Please imagine "Pomp and Circumstance" playing under the remainder.)

There was a time when guys got themselves all hot

and bothered *imagining* what was going on under a girl's sweater. Nowadays, a lot of you young gals prefer to "let it all hang out," parading your flesh all over MySpace in a kind of slutty one-upmanship that once upon a time took place only in brothels and the imaginations of GIs.

I guess what I'm trying to say is, before you lift up your shirt, pull off your undies, or loofah your room-mate's hoo-ha in the shower, all while making over-the-top "sexy faces" into the camera, pause for a moment and think. I know it's more difficult for some of you than others, especially after multiple shots of Purple Hooter, but please make an attempt. Sure, a lot of dumb-ass guys will think you are "hot," but they'll also probably think that you have chlamydia.

May God bless you and keep you . . . from acting like a ho. (Sorry, I couldn't resist.)

Sincerely,
Elizabeth Beckwith

I had better put aside this reader mail and get back on track. As you can see, step 2 is very involved, and an entire book could probably be written just on the art of brainwashing without being obvious and speaking disparagingly about people who do bad things.

Step 3 is a simple reinforcing of the togetherness of the "team." More hugs and more encouragement, which leads to more guilt if they go off track. Which is exactly what you want. Oh, and it will also lead to better self-esteem and all that good stuff, but the self-imposed guilt is what you are going for.

I would also suggest finding something that you can root for together as a family. Having a sports team that you can rally around is always helpful. When I was growing up, we had UNLV basketball. No matter what phase any of us were going through, we always had the common thread of cheering for the Rebels and rooting for the annihilation of their opponents. Although it reached obsessive levels and some considered our emotional investment in a college basketball program extreme, it was a magical thing for us as a family. I go into more detail about this in Chapter 8, "All for One and One for All."

Summary

We have now established the foundation of the Guilt and Manipulation philosophy (creating a team) and the steps necessary to create this foundation: (1) encouragement, (2) brainwashing, and (3) reinforcement. You can start applying these helpful techniques to your life immediately. Start slowly, building confidence as you go. You never want these methods to feel forced or phony. You've got to believe it to achieve it! (That sounds frighteningly familiar. Did Jesse Jackson say that, or did I just make it up on my own?)*

---

* Jesse, if you said this, I apologize for the lack of a proper footnote. If not, feel free to use this phrase and call it your own, I won't be upset.

Sweep It Under the Rug

So you have a schizophrenic third cousin whose "voices" told him to expose himself at the mini-mart. Is that any reason not to invite him to Christmas dinner? Many of you may be answering with a resounding "Yes! Of course a deranged sex offender shouldn't be invited to Christmas, Elizabeth!" Well, let's not be so shortsighted, people. It's not like I'm suggesting you dress him up as Santa and make everyone sit on his lap. Of course, you never leave your children alone with this relative and, since you have no problem talking badly about people in front of your kids, they know to beware. But at the same time, you will have provided your offspring with one of the most important gifts you can give them: a distant relative to mock as a family (not to mention a beautiful example of kindness and generosity of spirit). Let's face it: inside jokes about your own relatives are the glue that hold your nuclear family together.

Maybe because I was raised in an Italian Catholic family, sweeping things under the rug comes naturally to me. This cultural phenomenon can most likely be attributed to the combination of the Catholic tradition of forgiveness with the Italian tradition of pride, which together form the most basic incarnation of "Rug Sweepage." It seemed that no grudge was big enough to prevent a relative from sharing a meal with another family member who had wronged or disgusted them in some way. That didn't mean that some people didn't detest one another—I'm certain that they did—but these feuds never got in the way of the gluttonous consumption of food. Which reminds me: if you want your kids to be loyal, learn to be a good cook. All the kids I grew up with who claimed to hate their parents had crappy food in their house. Think about it: is your kid going to blow off dinner with the family if you're making his favorite lasagna? I don't think so.*

When I say, "Sweep it under the rug," I am not suggesting repression. When you repress something, you're pretending it didn't happen. When you sweep something under the rug, everyone knows what occurred, it's just that nobody talks about it—at least not in front of the main characters. Over the years these tales take on an urban legend–like quality as you whisper and giggle with your brother about your aunt who tried to run over your uncle, or your cousins who made out with each other. These common, albeit bizarre, bonds are more valuable than any family therapy could ever be. Embrace them, but be careful not to go blabbing all of your family secrets to outsiders; keep it in the family.† It's more special that way, and it's the right thing to do. Sweeping

---

* I discuss this in more detail in Chapter 6. For more help in this department, please see the Appendix, "Recipes to Keep Your Children From Running Away."

† This may seem a tad hypocritical since I seem to spill some secrets in this very book. Keep in mind that I am profiting from it, so that makes it okay.

things under the rug can be a little confusing at first, but with practice it will become as involuntary as breathing.

It is important to distinguish between the two types of Rug Sweepage. "Type 1 Rug Sweepage" is the act of intentionally keeping certain information from your children out of respect for everyone involved and as an attempt to prevent your child from being "confused" by unsettling facts. Invariably, one summer vacation, your kid will learn the truth from some older cousin and proceed to act as if he doesn't know. You'll know that he knows, but you'll pretend that you don't know that he knows. This charade will go on until one day when your child is in his early to mid-twenties and he says to you, "You know I knew that Aunt Christy wasn't a real masseuse, right?" Type 2 Rug Sweepage is when you carefully dole out certain key facts about certain relatives in an effort to protect your children from falling victim to or getting involved with said relative, while at the same time continuing on a seemingly cordial relationship with the person, never referencing her taboo history.

Both types of Rug Sweepage are valid and necessary. When you are a parent, there are certain things about certain relatives that you won't want to come outright and tell your children, but there are other things you'll want to "leak" to them in order to teach them right from wrong. For example, growing up I never knew that my cousin Jodie had been admitted to a mental institution or that my Uncle Johnny had gambled away his baby daughter (relax, he got her back five years later), but I *did* know that my cousin Paul was a con artist, and I heeded the advice, "Don't let him snow you!"

Why the discrepancy? Possessing the knowledge about my

Type 1 Rug Sweepage	Vs.	Type 2 Rug Sweepage
Uncle Leo is a hitman.		Uncle Leo killed a guy in a bar fight.
Type 1, because it is unlikely that Uncle Leo would be hired to "whack" your children, so the knowledge does not protect them from anything. It would be more dangerous if your children revealed this information to an outsider. Best if they don't know the truth about Uncle Leo until they are much older.		Lock your doors and don't ruffle Uncle Leo's feathers. Be nice to him when you run into him at family gatherings and give him a nice present at Christmas. But let your kids know that when the vodka comes out, it's best to let Uncle Leo win this round of Pictionary (heading for the door shortly thereafter: "Great game! See you later, Uncle Leo!")
Aunt Tina slept with her sixty-five-year-old boss.		Aunt Tina slept with her eighteen-year-old nephew.
Okay, so Aunt Tina is a little bit sleazy, but there is no need to tell your kids of her indiscretions. Better to keep this info under wraps; your children may look up to Aunt Tina, and you wouldn't want to glamorize her affair. The last thing you need is for your daughter to start fantasizing about the school principal in an unconscious effort to be like her hero, Aunt Tina.		This is a tricky one. If you don't have any sons, this would fall into Type 1, since there is no need for your daughters to have access to this information. However, if you have sons, this would fall under the umbrella of Type 2 Rug Sweepage—and this story will need to be leaked Dick Cheney style. You're going to have to throw Aunt Tina and the nephew in question under the bus on this one. Remember, the key here is to *leak* the information. Sitting your sons down to tell them the story is flat-out creepy.

Type 1 Rug Sweepage	Vs.	Type 2 Rug Sweepage
Cousin Donny is having a sexual identity crisis.		**Cousin Donny is an overtly sexual identity thief.**
Donny's got enough troubles without everybody whispering about him. If Donny wants to talk about whether he is going to become Donna, let him be the one to broach the subject.		Make sure everyone in the house is on high alert to keep their bosoms and their social security numbers under wraps when Donny comes to town. (Are you getting the hang of this yet?)

How to Leak

The best way to leak information to your family is through the art of *reverse eavesdropping*. Having a juicy telephone chat with your sister about Aunt Tina? Leave your bedroom door cracked and speak in "hushed tones"—if your kids hear you attempting to whisper, they will instantly be drawn to your conversation. Be sure to pepper the dialogue with phrases like "how disgusting" or "what sickies."

cousin Jodie or my Uncle Johnny wouldn't have "protected" me in any way; in fact, it probably would have frightened me—whereas the information about my cousin Paul was necessary to prevent me from being conned.

Sometimes the differences can be very subtle, but after careful thought it is easy to discern the difference.

The key here is not to shun the offending relative. Be generous and kind and don't exclude him from holiday dinners, always keeping your eyes open, of course. Then, after he leaves for the evening, "mention" a few things to your children; for example, "Your cousin Sammy looked good. Prison was the best thing that ever happened to him. He found Jesus *and* he learned how to shave. Let's pray to God he stays on the straight and narrow." Or, in some instances, do some "mentioning" before the evening begins; for example, "Your cousin Rocko is coming over. Hide your wallets and then help me grate the cheese."

You may be saying to yourself, "Yes, but, aren't there certain people who should never be invited over? Aren't some people simply unsafe to bring around your children?" Yes, of course, and I suspect you are the best judge of who those people are. Anyone who has a record of harming children or gives you the unshakable creeps should not be trusted in your home. But with careful prep work, a lot of low-lifes and weirdos can make acceptable visitors and, more important, provide your family with real examples of the devastation of those lifestyle choices.

If your children are clever, they will probably develop nicknames for some of these crazy characters. Although it is best not to join in on the ceremonious naming of the relatives out of the appearance of respect for the family, I would suggest turning a blind eye and allowing your kids to bond with each other through this creative and hilarious rite of passage. If they cross a line, you can interfere and reprimand them. Because you have given them the room necessary to mock and grow, when you do call them out for going too far they will feel appropriately ashamed and will be careful not to step over the line again.

Appropriate Nicknames for Inappropriate Relatives		
Relative	**Appropriate Nickname**	**Inappropriate Nickname**
Your chauvinistic, diabetic great-uncle, who weighs four hundred pounds, smokes foul-smelling cigars at holiday dinners despite the *Thank You for Not Smoking* sign, and squeezes all the girls too tightly, making comments like, "She's built like a brick shithouse."	Perv Griffin	Fat Bastard (This is an ad hominem attack and is never acceptable. The fact that he is fat has nothing to do with the fact that he is offensive. Maybe suggest "Sick Bastard" instead.)
Your cousin's innocent young wife who got an over-the-top boob job and suddenly dresses like she should be signing DVDs at the back of a porno convention.	Titty McGee	MILF (Come on, your kid can do better than that. Seriously, let's try to shut this nickname down already. Any reference involving a sexual act is off-limits. Although at this point, I would argue that "MILF" is more offensive for being lame and overused.)

Your uncle, a former pimp/drug lord, who found Jesus and won't stop trying to "save" perfectly innocent people at family gatherings.	The Jesus Pimp	Jesus the Pimp
Your brother-in-law the con man, who has an on-again, off-again relationship with cocaine. At rock bottom, he turned tricks for drug money.	Snow Man	Snow Blower

It is a fine line between dark family secrets and laughing and learning as a family. The point of this chapter is to encourage you to start thinking of ways to exploit the "bad" stuff for use as teaching tools and opportunities for bonding.

The following essay highlights some of my early experiences with discovering family secrets that had been "swept under the rug."

UP CLOSE AND PERSONAL
All Swept Up

I spent several summers on the East Coast while growing up, usually starting out with a week or two in Brooklyn with my Grandma Guido and then a week in Fairfield, Connecticut, with a favorite aunt and uncle and their four boys. I loved hanging out with my cousins. I had three older brothers of my own, and when I got to Connecticut, I had a fresh set of brothers to idolize. As a little girl, I relished the influences of my big brothers. Because of them I was a music snob by ten years old and was already heavily influenced by the comedy of *Saturday Night Live* and *Late Night with David Letterman*. My Connecticut cousins furthered this cultural education by introducing me to punk rock and the absurdity of professional wrestling. But they made their biggest impact on me by sharing their endless knowledge of our family.

My cousin Bobby seemed to know every secret there was to know about our relatives, and he delighted in revealing them to me.

"You know Aunt Luisa and Uncle Sal are first cousins, right?"

"What? No! Shut up!"

"I'm serious, Lizzie. Haven't you ever noticed that Angelo and Sam are a little off? Shallow gene pool."

Although I loved getting these scoops, I felt tortured by them. I spent most of my nights in Connecticut tossing and turning in my Holly Hobbie pajamas, trying to put the pieces together, my mind racing:

Of course my mother's cousins are weird! Why hadn't I realized it before? Angelo always did look a little funny, and he leans in so close when he talks to you. Of course his parents were first cousins! How else could you explain the unnatural way his cheeks puff out or the twisted look he gets on his face when he's eating? First cousins indeed! And Sam has that scary, monotone voice, still lives with his mother at age forty, and gives me a Bible every summer. I'm nine, how many

Bibles do I need? I hope I didn't just offend God. You know what I mean, God, right? I just don't think I need more than one Bible, as long as it's the Catholic version. By the way, is Jesus technically still Jewish? Does that make him a "Jew for Jesus"? I saw some of them on the subway with my grandma. Aren't they basically just Catholics who don't eat bacon?

How could I sleep with all of this on my mind? It was during this period that my first battles with paranoia began. I began panicking that my own dark secrets would become fodder for relatives.

"You know Elizabeth Ann wiped her boogers on the Malloys' car in the first grade, right?"

"Elizabeth Ann humps her pillow."

"Elizabeth Ann sleeps with her parents every night because she's scared the devil's going to get her."

I broke out into a sweat as I imagined my cousins doubled over, tears of laughter running down their cheeks. Terrified as I was of being exposed, I couldn't resist finding out more dirt about my relatives. Every night after dinner, we kids would make our way out onto the deck, pastries in hand, and a new set of secrets would be revealed.

Bobby even knew stuff about the other side of my family, people he'd met maybe once or twice. When I suspected that one of my relatives might secretly be gay, it was my cousin who confirmed it, laughing at me. "Of course he's gay, Lizzie. Everybody knows that. You're so cute how you think you're the only one who's figured it out."

"Everybody knows this?! Nobody told me."

"You're nine. They probably don't think you know what gay is."

"I know it means more than just happy."

"Anyway, nobody talks about it, but everybody knows. It's just one of those things."

Nobody talks about it, but everybody knows. As the years went on, I realized this applied to countless family secrets. When I was in my early twenties, it would be my brother Frank who would reveal these things to me.

"You know Mom and Dad sold chocolate penises at the candy store, right?"

"What? No! Shut up!"

"They kept them hidden, for special requests only."

"People *request* chocolate penises? Who are these people?"

In my parents' defense, their candy store was in Las Vegas. I never saw any chocolate penises when I worked there during my high school years, which renders me powerless to answer the age-old question, "Are dark chocolate penises bigger than their white chocolate counterparts?" However, the topless-woman lollipops were sold out in the open, and their nipples came in a variety of realistic, mouth-watering shades.

Amusing as a chocolate dildo may be, the most intriguing stories always involved my Uncle Johnny or his son, my cousin Nino. The stories about my uncle were dark and frightening, while the ones about Nino were dark and frighteningly hilarious, each one topping the next.

"You know Nino used to go jogging wearing only a beanie, right?"

"You know when he was thirteen, Nino had an affair with his Mom's wigmaker, right?"

"You know Nino made our dog lick his balls, right?"

No! My poor, sweet dog, Rebel. Molested by my own flesh and blood under our very roof. No wonder in his last years Rebel seemed so despondent. I hope to God Nino at least gave him a biscuit afterward.

Nino and my brothers went through adolescence together, so my siblings have countless tales of his legendary adventures. Entire volumes could be written about my good-looking, athletically gifted, intelligent cousin who used his gifts for evil.*

His father, Uncle Johnny, died of a drug overdose when I was two years old, but not before threatening to kill my entire family, "starting with the baby" (for the offense of not attending the funeral of his drug-addicted, nymphomaniac mistress). This "secret" was spilled to me during my college years. Terrible as it is to say, this information filled me with a twisted sense of pride. Imagine that, he was going to start his murderous rampage with little me! I couldn't have felt more special. He wasn't going to start with Frank or Jim or Patrick or my parents, he was going to "start with the baby"! I was practically a celebrity. I couldn't help wondering who my pallbearers would have been, since my brothers would have been dead too.

I have since realized that fantasizing about one's own funeral is the pinnacle of the combined traits of narcis-

---

* If you're reading this, Nino, you know I love you, and when I use the word *evil* it comes from a loving place. But seriously, did you have to seduce the dog?

sism and low self-esteem: "Everyone will love me . . . and I'll be dead."* But that is for me to work out.

Even after all of these years, my brother Frank or my cousin Bobby will still let slip some little bit of taboo family history. I still get the same uncomfortable buzz from it that I got when I was nine.

Discussion Questions

1. Did the knowledge about her relatives help Elizabeth or hurt her?

2. Which family secrets should you allow your child to discover?

3. Which relatives of yours are unsafe to leave alone with your pet?

Homework!

Start categorizing which of your family secrets fall into Type 1 Rug Sweepage and which fall into Type 2. This is a fun activity to do with your spouse. (It's kind of like scrapbooking, but with sex and drugs instead of die-cuts of birthday cakes.)

---

* Note to my loved ones: Is it asking too much for you to put together a video retrospective of me to play on a continuous loop during my wake? Please exclude any footage of me recreating the Beastie Boys' "Pass the Mic" video or any other footage in which my acne and/or eyebrows are out of control.

How Ready Are You to Turn Your Disturbing Family Secrets Into Laughter?

Take This Quiz and Find Out!

Rate the level of emotional distress that you might experience during the following scenarios:

1. While working on your family's ancestry, you discover that beloved Pop-Pop McGee, your dearly departed great-grandfather, was an old-time smut peddler known as the Larry Flynt of 1917.

    A.   None
    B.   Very little
    C.   Some
    D.   A lot

2. Your aunt and her new boyfriend have hit hard times and need a place to stay for a while. Your wonderful parents have agreed to take them in—putting them in separate rooms, of course—and they send you out to the car to help with the luggage. When you open the trunk, you discover that it is full of sex toys.

    A.   None
    B.   Very little
    C.   I don't know whether to laugh, cry, or steal a dildo.
    D.   I am beyond disturbed.

3. While you are visiting your cousin in his new mental institution, he confides in you that he has always had a crush on you. He begins to weep uncontrollably. While you console him, you suddenly realize he has been pleasuring himself the entire time.

    A.   I'm kind of turned on right now.
    B.   Very little
    C.   Some
    D.   Police!

4. Your Uncle Barry has started his own religion and tries to strong-arm you into having your wedding at his "church." When you tell him you are uncomfortable getting married in a place called the Church of Barry, he tries to run you over.

    A.   None
    B.   Very little
    C.   Some
    D.   Holy Mary, mother of God, help me!
    E.   Holy Barry, brother of God, help me!

5. You are coming home from a party late one night, when you think you spot your Uncle Jake's car. You start to change lanes to say hello, when he pulls over and picks up what appears to be a prostitute.

    A.   This is awesome, I'm totally going to blackmail him.

B. Maybe he's just giving that poor young girl a ride . . . . a poor young girl in stilettos whose giant ass is bursting out of a tiny, metallic G-string.

C. Some

D. A lot

Interpreting the Results

Unless you are a sociopath or in serious denial, you most likely answered C or D (with an occasional B thrown in) to most of these unsettling scenarios. That is healthy and perfectly normal. You were most likely reading these as if the events were unfolding right before your very eyes, so you were appalled, and rightly so.

Now I would like you to get into your time machine and blast off to ten years from now. It is holiday time and you are gathered around the fire with your siblings and a couple of favorite cousins. You've had a couple of glasses of wine and you are all trying to one-up each other with disturbing family stories.

There is an old adage that "comedy is tragedy plus time." That will never seem truer than when the thing that you had once thought would scar you for life, the image of your psychotic cousin fondling himself in a strait-jacket, is now leaving everyone in stitches. Your sister just shot wine out of her nose, she's laughing so hard. Feels good, doesn't it?

When life gives you lemons, make lemonade. When life gives you an uncle who enjoys screwing hookers in his car, make lemonade again, but add a little vodka to it and have a few laughs at his expense.

Summary

Family secrets can be helpful learning tools. You will teach your children compassion by not excluding people for their crimes, while at the same time providing your kids with real-world examples of the dangers of making poor choices. And, if used correctly, family secrets can be a lot of fun. Sometimes it will be up to you to leak crucial information to your children, but more often than not, other people will do your dirty work for you. Sometimes people will reveal things to your children that you wish they had never known, but that comes with the territory. Take comfort in the fact that your kids are bonding with their family as they gossip about the misadventures of others.

With practice, you will learn to sweep up certain secrets more tidily than others as you organize the world that lives beneath your rug. Remember, before your kids can begin to experience guilt, they need to understand how you view the world. Allowing them to overhear your commentary of other people's dirty laundry is a helpful tool.

3

How to Scare the Crap Out of Your Child (in a Positive Way)

INT. FAMILY KITCHEN—EVENING

A FATHER sits at the table reading the newspaper while eating cookies. His DAUGHTER, a cute college girl, walks in.

DAUGHTER

Hi, Daddy.

FATHER

Hi, sweetheart. Did you have some cookies?

DAUGHTER

Nah. I'm on a diet.

FATHER

You're too damn thin as it is. You're gonna waste away.

The father spills crumbs down his shirt as he takes a bite of another cookie.

FATHER

   Oh well, more for me.

DAUGHTER

   So, my friends and I are thinking of going to T.J. for the weekend.

FATHER

   T.J.?

DAUGHTER

   Tijuana.

FATHER

   Tijuana?! What the hell would you want to go there for?

DAUGHTER

   (guilty)

   I don't know. It's supposed to be fun.

FATHER

   You'd just better be careful.

DAUGHTER

   We will. Of course, we will.

FATHER

   You have no rights when you're over there. No rights. Let me tell you, those Federales will rob you, rape you, and leave you to rot in a Mexican jail, all because you didn't have the forty bucks to pay them off.

DAUGHTER

   Well—

FATHER

   You'd better bring an extra forty bucks with you and set it aside as bribe money.

DAUGHTER

   Okay.

FATHER
> Better yet, two sets of forty bucks. In case you get stopped twice.

DAUGHTER
> So, eighty bucks?

FATHER
> Yeah, but in two separate parts of your wallet. They have to think that forty is all you've got. You understand?

DAUGHTER
> I . . . think so. Anyway, I'll bring the phone number for the American embassy, in case I'm mistreated.

FATHER
> (laughing)
> You think you get a phone call? This isn't the United States we're talking about.

DAUGHTER
> Oh.

FATHER
> And don't make eye contact with anybody down there. You make eye contact, you might as well have a big target on your back.

DAUGHTER
> Well, I mean . . . we're probably not even going. We were just, you know, talking about maybe going.

FATHER
> Oh, I thought you had already decided.

DAUGHTER
> Nah. I mean, with those Federales and everything . . . you'd have to be nuts to go.

FATHER
Smart girl.

The daughter grabs a cookie and starts munching.

The preceding scene was an example of how simple it can be to frighten your child out of doing something without having to "lay down the law." The father in this scenario never once tells his daughter she can't go; he merely "mentions" the terrible things that could happen to her in a foreign land.

Notice how he opens with the comment, "What the hell would you want to go there for?" This is a very effective manipulation tool. The girl instantly feels ashamed as the image of her drunk, under-aged self making out with a hot stranger flashes through her mind. Terrified that the same image may be flashing through her father's mind, the kid wants to crawl under a rock and die. Mission accomplished.

If the father had said, "What do you want to do, drink and make out with guys?" the daughter probably would have gotten defensive. "What the hell do you want to go there for?" puts the burden on the daughter to defend her lousy decision making while making her feel ashamed. Remember, when you are a parent, shame is your friend! You need to let go of the modern notion that "you should never make your child feel ashamed." Are you kidding me? That's the whole point of shame: to make children feel terrible about themselves—in a positive way, of course.

The father then goes a step further: "You'd just better be careful." This conveys a casual acceptance of the daughter's plans while at the same time expressing concern and obvious disapproval. Even though the father is "accepting" because his daughter is a legal adult, he broadcasts disapproval. This type of mixed message is a very effective way to invade your child's developing psyche. In other words, a home run. Once again, the father puts the burden on the daughter to question how good an idea the trip is. This warning, of course, is followed by cautionary tales of the danger that could follow. Next thing you know, the daughter has changed her mind about the trip and is shoving a cookie in her face, making the father victorious on two levels.

The important thing to note is that the daughter ultimately made the decision not to go to T.J. on her own. Again, the "appearance of freedom" is at work here. Instead of making broad statements like, "You are forbidden from doing that, young lady," the father empowered his daughter to make the right decision with the one-two punch of fear and self-loathing.

To give you a better understanding of this form of manipulation, I have listed some popular parenting responses to several different scenarios and have suggested some more effective alternatives.

Scenario	Popular Response	Alternative
"I want a pony."	"You're not getting a pony, and that's final!"	"What the hell do you want a pony for? The thing will be crapping all over the place, and God forbid it tramples someone to death. I'm not so sure about this pony business."
"I'm thinking of getting a tattoo."	"You're not getting a tattoo and that's final!"	"A tattoo is forever, you know. You want to be ninety years old with a sun on your lower back? Remember what happened to Gary up the block? He got a tattoo, and next thing you know the poor kid's got hepatitis."
"I want to move in with my boyfriend/ girlfriend."	"Over my dead body!"	"Are you going to have your own room or are you planning to share a bed?" If your kid respects you at all, he or she has probably turned a deep shade of crimson by now, mortified that this is surprising to you. If it's not really shocking, you need to do a little acting here.

All roads lead to death. That was my mantra as a child. I had completely forgotten about it until recently, when my cousin Bethany reminded me. In Chapter 1 I briefly mentioned how important it is to weave the fear of death into your exchanges with your children. As you can see in the examples of alternative responses to popular requests, two out of three of them involve death or disease, and the third involves shame, which, for many, is worse than dying.

Let me drive home the point that when I suggest "scaring" your child, it is through cautionary tales, not through threats of "what I would do to you if . . ." Not that threats are never necessary; sometimes they absolutely are. Usually for small things like, "If you throw that food one more time, I'm taking your plate away." Threats of that nature can be very effective when used correctly as opposed to "If you don't stop yelling, I'll rip out your voice box," which is over the top with the suggestion of violence and impossible to follow through with unless you are a sadistic maniac, in which case, seek help now. The threat of violence should be directed only at objects, not at people. For example, "Throw the doll one more time and she goes in the trash compactor!" as opposed to "Throw the doll one more time and *you're* going in the trash compactor." Although I don't think either threat is a good idea for obvious reasons, I'm just saying if you're feeling out of control, aim your rage at a thing, not your child. Which leads me to my next point.

The golden rule with threatening is, *Never make a threat unless you're willing to follow through with it.* This is a crucial rule, and it is no accident that it is also one of the guiding principles of the Mafia. You must be careful before you make statements like, "Do it one more time and the TV goes out the window!" Because they may just "do it again," and guess what? The TV *has to* go out the window. Even if the window is closed, you have no choice but to send that television spiraling through the double-paned glass. Why? Because you said you would, and you are the head of this family! This is no time for a weak, bumbling "I didn't mean *literally*" rationale for your lack of follow-through. Did John Gotti speak in metaphors? I am not suggesting you go through life throwing appliances through glass like a lunatic, which is obviously dangerous and expensive; just don't *say* that you will if you aren't willing to follow through.

Like most of the ideas in this book, I learned this important rule from my mother, a woman who murdered a basketball. Family legend has it that one day my mother had a terrible headache and was lying down on her bed when my brothers started playing a loud and aggressive game of basketball in the yard outside her window. She went outside to tell them to stop, and they did . . . for about five minutes, and then the ball started bouncing again. Upset, my mother went back outside to tell them to stop. Once again, the game only stopped for moments until the loud bouncing of the ball echoed through my mother's room. This time when she came back out, she told them, "Do it one more time, and I'll kill the basketball." My brothers, thinking this absurd notion was hilarious, ignored her request and went back to their game. The next time my mother came out, she was holding a giant butcher knife. Like a gangster in a prison fight, my mother inflicted the basketball with multiple stab wounds.

Whenever she is asked about this story, my mother says, "As soon as the words came out of my mouth, I regretted them, because I knew I'd have to follow through if they did it again. I was praying they wouldn't do it again; I didn't want to have to kill the basketball. That's why you have to be careful when you make a threat. I learned my lesson." Rest in peace, Spalding, rest in peace.

Safety

The motivation behind frightening your children is to keep them safe. Whether they are young adults traveling abroad or small children crossing the street for the first time, you want them to be educated about the dangers that exist in the world. Kids need to know *why* you don't want them to play outside without supervision: "Someone could kidnap you and leave you to die in the desert!" A lot of parents are funny about this. They don't want their child to do something, so they will tell them they are not allowed to. But because they are uncomfortable with the idea of frightening their child, they won't explain why. They are actually scared to scare their child! They somehow think that the image of a madman disguised as the ice cream man, shoving their kid into the deep freeze, is unhealthy for a child to fixate on. Perhaps it is, but in a *good* way.

Children are born innocent; ironically, in order to preserve that innocence you need to teach them to be a little bit cynical and untrusting. You want your kids to begin to look at the world around them with some skepticism; this way when a perv shows up at the park claiming he has lost a puppy, your kids will immediately think to themselves, "This guy is full of shit" and run for the hills.

Shame: It Really Works

The other day I was talking on the phone with my cousin Bethany. We were talking about my book, and she told me a great story about her thirteen-year-old daughter, Katie. Bethany's kids know that they have to call and check in with her when they are out with their friends, and let her know if they are changing locations or if they are going to be late coming home.

Katie came home from school the other day and said, "Mom, all my friends were asking me what you would do if I didn't call and check in with you. I told them that you wouldn't do anything, and they said, 'Then why do you have to call?'

"I told them, 'You don't understand; my mom would be so disappointed in me and I'd feel so, so . . .' I couldn't think of the word then, but I just thought of it. I'd feel so ashamed!"

Well done, Bethany. Well done.

UP CLOSE AND PERSONAL
Fear and Self-Loathing in Las Vegas—
Great Moments in Dread and Shame

One time I commented to my friend Brian Liscek that he looks very young for his age. He replied, "I'm well preserved from living in a cocoon of fear most of my life." This has since become one of my all-time favorite quotes.

A large portion of my youth was spent in a state of terror. Terrified that I'd get kidnapped. Terrified that my Halloween candy was chocolate-dipped razor blades. Terrified that I'd electrocute myself if I bathed in the same room as a hair dryer. I have my parents to thank for this. Let's look at some highlights.

I'll never forget the Christmas that I got a Holly Hobbie Easy-Bake oven. It was unique; unlike the modern-looking Easy-Bake ovens everyone else had, mine looked like an old-time stovetop, something right out of *Little House on the Prairie*. I couldn't have loved it more and was so excited to bake some treats in my vintage-looking oven, imagining I worked in a Depression-era boardinghouse, boosting morale with my homemade goodies. I could not wait to get started.

My mom and I baked one cake together, and then she cut the cord off and told me to "pretend from now on." What? No! To this day that was the most delicious cake I have ever eaten if only because I would never be permitted to make another one. Why did my mother do this? Simple. She didn't want me to try to bake one alone and electrocute myself, or set the house on fire, or some disastrous combination of the two. She was right. From that moment on I set out on a crusade to warn all the other little girls in my class of the potential dangers of the Easy-Bake oven.

"Your mom really should cut the cord off."

"Why? I love my oven. The cakes are soooo good!"

"It's just as fun to pretend," I'd say, trying to convince myself.

"My mom lets me bake. Why do you care?"

"Because I don't want you to blow yourself up!" I'd huff off, dreaming of the tiny, delicious chocolate cake that would never again touch my lips and then quickly shifting gears, deciding that other people must have mothers who are either terrible or stupid.

To this day I have never climbed a tree because my mother told me I could break my neck. It hardly seemed worth the risk. I mean, why would you want to sit on a branch anyway when there was a perfectly comfortable couch in the house, conveniently parked in front of the television and mere steps from a drawer full of cookies? I looked out the window at my neighbors carelessly risking their lives and had another cookie, crossing myself as I dunked it into my milk.*

For my sixth birthday, someone sent me a shirt with my name on it. I was thrilled to have something with my name on it. I had never had anything like it before. I wore the shirt once to the grocery store with my mother, and then my mom made it disappear forever.

"What happened to my *Elizabeth* shirt?"

"I don't like you wearing that shirt, honey."

"Why?"

"Because you might be wearing it one day and you'll forget that you have it on and some stranger will come up to you, read your shirt, and say, 'Hi, Elizabeth, your mom told me to pick you up today.' And because he knows your name, you might believe him and end up getting kidnapped. Shirts like that aren't safe."

---

* For you non-Catholics out there, "crossing yourself" is when you make the sign of the cross. It can be very habit forming. I do it not only at the beginning and end of prayers, but also whenever an ambulance goes by, when I pass a cemetery, or if a terrible thought involving death pops into my mind—which, admittedly, is more often than is healthy.

Several weeks later I saw Suzy Wong wearing a *Suzy* shirt at the parish picnic. I felt I had a moral obligation to warn her of the potential danger.

"You'd better just be careful in that shirt."

"What are you talking about?"

I tried my best to explain my mother's theory to Suzy. She looked at me like I was nuts.

"I'd never go somewhere with someone I didn't know," Suzy countered.

"Yeah, but, you'd *think* he must know you, because he knows your name."

"No, I wouldn't." Suzy skipped off, licking her snow cone.

"I just don't want you to get kidnapped!" I called out after her. I didn't want to add that she shouldn't be skipping with that snow cone, since the bottom was conical and if she fell she could poke her eye out. There's just no getting through to some people.

In the third grade, the school principal sent a letter home to all of the parents, warning them of a new scare. Apparently at another school, there had been an incident in which stickers laced with LSD had been passed out to unsuspecting students. This was at the height of the sticker album craze. My mom sat me down.

"Has anyone given you any stickers?"

"Just the ones I've been trading at school."

"Don't take any with Mickey Mouse on them. And don't take any stickers from strangers. Ever."

"Why? What's happening?"

"Some bad people are giving kids Mickey Mouse stickers

that have been dipped in LSD. It's a drug that makes you hallucinate and lose your mind. All you have to do is touch them and the drugs get in your bloodstream."

"Oh my God!" I immediately began panicking at the idea of it.

The next day at recess, I cased the playground for the sickos who were trying to poison us with their dope. I saw a suspicious guy in an Adidas tracksuit hanging out on the sidewalk outside of our school. Could this be our guy? I was just about to alert the mom on playground duty when I saw a group of first-graders trading stickers near the tetherball pole. I ran over.

"None of those are Mickey Mouse, are they?" I asked, out of breath.

"No, they're mostly Hello Kitty . . . Oh wait, here's a Mickey Mouse." The little girl pointed to a sticker of Mickey waving from behind the protective clear plastic of her sticker album.

"Oh my God! Didn't your parents get the memo?" I shouted. The girl nervously stared at me, confused. "Did you touch this sticker?" I demanded, like one of the detectives I'd seen on *Hill Street Blues*. "You might be high right now. I'm trying to help you! Answer the question." The girl started bawling and ran over to the playground mom.

Had she just told me that she had gotten it at the stationery store at the mall, we could have avoided the entire uncomfortable exchange in which the playground mom made me feel like a villain, instead of acknowledging that I was the only student in the entire school who took this sticker scare seriously. As for the guy in the tracksuit, the verdict is still out on him.

So, yes, like my friend Brian I have spent a good deal of my life afraid. Although mine was less a "cocoon of fear" and more of a rocket of fear, in which I blasted off to any location in which I believed it necessary to impose my fears onto others.

Shame

The only thing that comes close to surpassing my many frightened moments is my ability to feel ashamed at the drop of a hat, particularly with things of a sexual nature.

My first kiss was at Caesars Palace. It was nighttime and it was just the two of us sitting out by the pool. I didn't like the guy, but I really wanted to get my first kiss out of the way. He leaned in for the kill, and then it happened. It was awkward and awful. It felt like I had a caterpillar in my mouth.

As our teeth clumsily clanked together, I hoped it wasn't obvious that I didn't know what I was doing, and then he looked at me funny and asked, "Have you ever done this before?"

I made a face like he was insane and said, "Of course. I'm just not used to kissing someone with braces."

Later that night he tried poorly to be smooth, like some kind of terrible high school production of Don Juan. We were on the people-mover together and as we passed the tiny hologram of Caesar, he whispered in my ear, "Tell me what you want." He whispered it in an embarrassing version of a seductive voice, the rubber bands from his braces grazing my earlobe. I was repulsed. "Tell me what you want." Tell you what I want? I'm thirteen years old. I spent the entire summer trying to build a time machine. What I want is a vessel that can travel past the speed of light. Maybe then I can go back to when this evening began and stay home and watch *Falcon Crest* with my mom.

It's not that I'm not a passionate person, or that I wasn't a romantic kid; I was. I had fantasized about my first kiss on many occasions. But none of those fantasies involved hatching a hasty plot with my friend Andrea to ensure that my first kiss occurred before my first day of high school. The plot basically boiled down to, "This guy who likes me has a friend named Bill. They want to meet us at Omnimax."

The next morning, Bill called my house.

"Who was that on the phone?" my mother wanted to know.

I tried to be casual. "Just a guy I got together with last night."

I can't remember what my mom was cooking at the moment, but she instantly stopped what she was doing, and although she was standing several yards from where I was sitting, it was as if she were suddenly in extreme close-up.

"A guy you what?"

"Got together with."

"What's that supposed to mean?"

"Nothing. We just kissed," I said, as though this type of thing happened all the time, which, in retrospect, was not the best way to play it. But there I sat, painting myself as some sort of harlot.

I was already ready to die when my dad walked into the kitchen.

My mom put it right out there just as casually as I had. "Lizzie kissed a boy last night." I immediately wanted to impale myself on the nearest sharp object.

"It was nothing! I don't even like him. It was my first kiss!" I ran out of the room, and the next time Bill called, I pretended I wasn't home.

I made it through most of high school without a boyfriend. I "got together" with my fair share of boys, but I never had a real boyfriend, so I avoided getting myself into situations where there was pressure to touch anyone's genitals.

That all changed senior year, when I began dating Oscar. It didn't take long for me to get yelled at during a make-out session. "Why won't you just touch it? It's not a big deal!"

I had been dreading this moment. I racked my brain for a clever retort, something that was cute, maybe even sexy, and, ideally, something that didn't make me sound like a terrified prude. But I was nervous, and all I could come up with was, "My mother would kill me." That pretty much did the trick.

This would be a perfect place to include some hilarious college stories, but my parents are still alive and I'd like to keep it that way. See, even to this day, I am worried about what they think of me. It amazes me that there can be so many people who do not have this issue.

In a similar vein, I have always been in awe of people who are sexually free. How are they so relaxed and uninhibited? How does anyone have casual sex at all, let alone without sobbing immediately following orgasm? Do they not have that part of their brain that makes their parents, three brothers, Grandma, and Jesus appear in the room the minute their pants come off? Furthermore, how can you even enjoy sex if you don't feel terrible about what you're doing the entire time? As a Catholic, I find this very confusing.

Even if I felt otherwise, I would never admit it, because that would make me feel, you know, ashamed.

Discussion Questions

1. What are some fears that are healthy to impose upon your own children?
2. Wasn't that playground mom kind of a bitch?
3. What steps can you take to ensure that your kids experience shame?

Homework!

Remember, fear is your friend! The next time your child asks permission to participate in an activity that you are uncomfortable with, try sprinkling the fear of death into your response. (They may still participate, but they will be on high alert and will be less likely to hurt themselves or others.) For example, if they say, "I want to go on a ski trip with my friends," your response could be, "Make sure you take a lesson, otherwise you could ski into a tree and die!" or "Just be careful; don't drink beer in the hot tub, you could fall asleep and drown. Don't laugh, it happens!"

Summary

When you are manipulating your offspring to make the right choices (that is, doing what you want them to do), it is important to plant the seed of fear in them. Instead of forbidding them from participating in something, let them decide not to do it on their own, by making the activity sound like a recipe for death or dismemberment. If they respect you, they will feel like fools for even considering taking part.

4

Don't Worry About the Mean Kid's Feelings, Make Your Own Kid Feel Better

Let's be honest, there are a lot of assholes in this world, and that includes children. How often have you been to the playground and seen some little monster taunting and pushing another kid off the monkey bars and thought to yourself, "What a little shit." If the parent is nowhere to be found, and my child is on the receiving end of the abuse, I like to use this as an opportunity to "save" a child before he goes further to the dark side. How? By using simple mind games to manipulate the little bastard. By the time I am finished breaking him down, I can almost guarantee he will be the nicest boy on the playground. The next thing you know, the kid will worship my child and me in a kind of preschool Stockholm syndrome that makes me beam with pride. My mother taught me well. Some people call it "crossing a line"; I call it rehabilitating a child. You can thank me later.

Does every foe of your child deserve to be taken down in this way? No. Some kids are just "testing" their boundaries and don't mean any harm. The ones who are in need of aggressive manipulation tactics are the overt playground bullies and toddler queen bees (aka "bitches"—yes, a four-year-old can be a bitch, but with your help she doesn't have to stay one).

I had my first altercation/rehabilitation with one of these kids when my son, Michael, was about eighteen months old. Her name was Tess, she was four years old, and she was from hell. Michael was having fun on the sandbox fire truck. Tess (whose name I did not know at the time, but would learn in a few moments) came running over, screaming, "That's my fire truck! You can't be in there! It's mine! Get out!" Michael, confused by this girl's terrifying demands, stared at me for help while Tess shot daggers through him.

I looked to my left and I looked to my right, and saw no parental figures in the immediate vicinity. I thought to myself, "It's on, bitch."

"Get him out! That's my fire truck and he can't be in it!" Tess reiterated her message.

At this point, a lot of modern parents, knee deep in the battle of politeness, would turn to their child and say, "Michael, why don't we let this little girl have a turn?" If Tess had asked sweetly, I would have done the same. But guess what? Tess was a demon in hot-pink Crocs, so Mommy's not gonna play that game. (If Tess had been two or even three, it would have been a little different; a lot of kids that age are still struggling to grasp the concept of sharing, but Tess was four. Sorry, but, she should have known better.)

"Actually, this isn't your fire truck. It belongs to the park and it's for everybody to use. Michael is using it right now.

There's another steering wheel if you'd like to play too." Ball is in your court, kid.

"It doesn't belong to everyone! It's my fire truck!"

"I don't know what to tell you. It belongs to the park. It's for everyone to share."

Tess reluctantly got into the truck, checking my son to the boards as she climbed on top of him to get to the other steering wheel. "Well, he can't have any of my crackers, then!" Tess stated, clutching her filthy bag of Goldfish crackers. Michael, who had not even noticed her crackers prior to this moment, turned to me and said, "Cracker, Mommy? Cracker pease!"

"Oh, Michael," I began, my profile inches from Tess's face, as I pretended she no longer existed, "you don't want any of *those* crackers; we have better food at our house. Besides, her hands were all over them," I said, making a disgusted face.

"Ants weren't all over them!" Tess said, misunderstanding me.

I looked her right in the eye and corrected her. "No, sweetie, your *hands*."

If this had been a nice kid, my comments and tone would have caused her to crumble and therefore would have been cruel and ineffective. But this was not a nice kid. This girl was a pain-in-the-ass devil child who wanted more than her share. And since, unlike Willy Wonka, I could not summon a team of Oompa-Loompas to sing to her about her faults, I would have to use my own methods. Turns out, they worked.

"My name's Tess, I'm four years old, and he can have some of my crackers!" Tess called out in a sunny voice. "Here, have some!" she said, shoving the bag toward my son, both of them smiling from ear to ear. Even though I was still turned off by

Tess's dirty crackers, saying a silent prayer that my son wasn't reaching into a bag full of whooping cough, I was thrilled with Tess's turnaround.

"Oh, isn't that nice, Michael? That is so nice of you, Tess. Thank you!" I said, more than thrilled to serve up a little positive reinforcement to my new best friend, Tess. The next thing I know, an exasperated woman, who I assumed was Tess's mother, came jogging over. "Is everything all right over here? Are you being nice, Tess?" Tess looked at me, and I sensed her panicking over which direction I might go with this.

"Oh, yes! She was just sharing her crackers with my son. She's a real character, isn't she?" I offered, laughing casually. I felt so powerful, like a Clint Eastwood character from the 1970s. I couldn't help but imagine Clint in the role of me. I could just see him dressed in raggedy velour sweatpants, a vintage T-shirt, and artsy eyeglasses, delivering lines like, *We're a team now, kid; you play nice and I'll have your back every time, Tess. But return to your old ways and I'll be your worst nightmare.*

Notice that the first step I took was to correct Tess's "misconception" about the fire truck. "Misconception" in quotes because I believe she knew the reality, but chose to pretend otherwise. I informed her that it was not, in fact, hers, thereby giving her the opportunity to shift gears. When she taunted my son with her filthy crackers, I ignored her and addressed my son. After all, she had no obligation to give my son any of her snacks, so I had nothing to say to her. More important, I wanted to instantly build my son up by letting him know that we have better food at our house. This accomplished two things: first and foremost, it transformed my son from feeling sad and rejected to feeling happy and superior. Secondly, it made Tess a nicer girl. How? I'm not a hundred percent certain of the psychology behind it, but I suspect it has something to do with the idea that bullies are attracted to people who don't take their shit. Or perhaps by teasing her with the idea of our mysterious pantry and the delectable treats that await within it, she wanted to be "in" with us. All I know is, it works. (Then, of course, when Tess's behavior took a turn for the better, I reinforced her good behavior with praise.)

What did I learn from this experience? When another kid is hurting your child, the most important thing to do is to make your child feel better. That sounds obvious, but we live in a time when people are terrified of confrontation, even if it is a preschooler we are talking about. Sometimes making your kid feel better requires belittling the mean kid right in front of their face. Once your skills are highly developed, there is nothing wrong with manipulating another person's child for the greater good of the culture at large. Just be careful not to abuse this power by accidentally using it on a child who is just testing her boundaries.

How can you tell the difference? If the kid is just testing his boundaries, it may not be obvious to you right away (especially if you are new to this technique). When in doubt, you should assume that it is just a kid testing his limits. Rest assured, when a nightmare child in need of your manipulative rehab comes along, there will be little doubt.

Ridicule

Whenever I was ridiculed as a youth, like many other parents, my folks turned it into a compliment. "She's just jealous." "He probably has a crush on you." "She wishes she had hips like yours. Childbirth will be a lot easier for you, let me tell you." This last one was doubly effective, since it made me feel better about myself while at the same time sending a subliminal reminder that childbirth was by its nature painful, and thus sex should be avoided at all costs.

Old-fashioned as this notion is, I believe in it. Even though your child will probably never believe that the kid shooting spitballs in her hair while shouting "pizza face" has a crush on her, there is an undeniable comfort in the fact that your parents are willing to stretch the truth just to make you feel better about yourself.

Typical Childhood Taunt	Parental Interpretation
"Out of my way, nerd."	"He's just jealous because you're so smart."
"You know you have a mustache, right?"*	"It's so obvious he's in love with you." Or "She's just jealous because you're so gorgeous."
"Your hair looks like a bush"	"He wishes he had hair like yours; he'll be bald by twenty-five."

It is time once again for the "Up Close and Personal" portion of our chapter (*insert theme music here*). In this episode we see

---

* Um . . . this is "typical," isn't it?

young Lizzie Beckwith experiencing the highs and lows of high school. As always, discussion questions will follow.

(*fade out theme music*)

UP CLOSE AND PERSONAL
Food in My Face

By my junior year of high school I believed I had really come into my own. I considered myself an artist and a thinker, a quirky trailblazer, a character out of a Bob Dylan song (but not the one where he sings, "One day you'll be in the ditch, flies buzzin' around your eyes . . ."). I was certain that the jerks at my high school secretly saw me this way as well. I understood that they couldn't admit out loud that I was amazing and talented and "pretty in an offbeat, exotic, not like the vanilla cheerleaders at our school" kind of way. They weren't confident enough to take that social risk. But I was satisfied knowing that one day they would reflect back on their teenaged years and wonder, "What ever happened to Elizabeth Beckwith? I'll bet she's doing amazing things right now. Boy, she really seemed like a special kind of genius. Why didn't I ask her out when I had the chance?" Of course, by that time I would have used my endless talents to propel me to an untouchable superstardom, and they'd *know* what I was up to. This all put a spring in my step as I anonymously walked the halls of my small Catholic high school.

In my freshman and sophomore years I had been caught up in the social scene. Having not been terribly popular in eighth grade, I was relieved to find that boys actually liked me and to be invited to the same parties as the people who ruled the campus. I soaked it all up along with the various candy-flavored alcoholic beverages that went along with it.

By junior year I was "over it." A lot of this had to do with witnessing the metamorphosis of my best friend, Bonnie. Bonnie and I had been inseparable. She was just like me, but angrier. Four years earlier we had been wheeling a Radio Flyer wagon full of spray paint and stencils around the neighborhood selling our services as curb painters. Well, not the entire curb; we offered to repaint the address numbers on the side of your curb. Our hook was that we used fluorescent orange paint so that "you can see it in the dark!" We used our profits to save up for the parts necessary to make our dream come true—to build a time machine so that we could go back to 1965 and become the best friends/girlfriends of the Beatles.

But by sophomore year Bonnie had fully immersed herself in the popularity race, and for a while I awkwardly struggled to keep up with her. It was no use. She was better at it than I was, and she knew it. Slowly my partner in crime was turning into my nemesis as she poisoned the minds of boys who were interested in me by saying things like, "Why would you like Liz? Liz is a nerd with a big ass." What was I supposed to say? "My mom says that men like that! Big asses, I mean, not nerds." That was the end. I decided that Bonnie had sold her soul, and we had a painful breakup. A breakup that involved a lot of nasty answering machine messages that included statements like, "What the fuck, Lizzie? Don't call up and fucking leave a bunch of fucking bad words on my answering machine!" And "Why don't you just go hang out with your Maureen friends!" This latter was a reference to a group of girls that I had recently begun hanging out with, the leader of which was Maureen, a girl Bonnie and I had both been friendly with in eighth grade.

Like someone on the rebound after a terrible breakup, I jumped headfirst into my new social circle. I loved my Maureen friends. We shared a whole new set of inside jokes, the kind that Bonnie and I used to share back when we were the same person. My Maureen friends "got me." Yep, junior year I believed I had returned to my roots. I felt like St. Francis, abandoning all material things and running through Assisi nude in protest of all the people caught up in the rat race. (Although if anyone actually ran through Bishop Gorman nude, they would be expelled, which always struck me as ironic since we watched *Brother Sun, Sister Moon* every year at Easter time.) I got serious about keeping a journal and filled it with poetic entries about all the fake-olas at my high school, many of which included some turn of the phrase, "She's just a shell! A shell of a person!" Or the always classic "I HATE YOU!" scrawled in giant, angry letters.

What I'm building toward here is that I had achieved a sort of high school enlightenment, and in the midst of my angst toward all the fake-olas I had found happiness. Through channeling my hostile feelings I had attained a peaceful satisfaction, and I was buzzing along merrily until the day a giant burrito hit me in the face.

Well, it didn't start with a burrito. It started with much smaller, less aggressive foods. Grapes. Pretzels. French fries. At one end of the cafeteria table sat my Maureen friends and I, and at the other end sat the asshole of the universe, Chad Pratt, and his friends. The previous fall Chad had tried to kiss me after a football game, and I rebuffed him. Now he had taken to throwing food at my Maureen friends and me while calling me names like *whore*. It's always great to be called a whore for *not* making out with somebody. I would have mocked him for this, but I was pretty sure Chad Pratt was missing the sarcasm chip.

The day things took a turn for the worse was the day I decided to take a stand. Some of the other Maureen friends giggled and flirted as the food came flying over. Perhaps they had the right idea; maybe the whole thing was just adolescent flirtation disguised as abuse. But I wasn't having it. I am not wired to find things like that cute. I can't remember exactly what I said or did—I'm sure it wasn't anything particularly brilliant—but whatever it was, it was enough to elevate me to the status of sole target. And that's when the heavy artillery started to come out.

One day a burrito to the head, the next day a dish of spaghetti placed on my seat at the last moment. Once I tried to fight back by throwing my milkshake at them, but I misfired and accidentally hit an innocent fat girl at the next table. Lunchtime became a living hell. I dreaded lunch and the three periods that followed, where I was forced to finish the school day looking like a walking Soup Plantation. Several people suggested that I simply move to a different table, and they probably had the right idea, but I couldn't do it. I wasn't going to give up my seat because "the man" was disrespecting me! Splattered with sloppy joe meat, I stuck to my guns, fancying myself the Rosa Parks of my high school.

One day at rehearsals for the school play (*Spoon River Anthology*, if you're interested) my drama teacher asked about my stains. I started to make a joke about it, but then my voice began to shake and I started crying. Now I really felt pathetic. The funny girl in tears. What a cliché! My new-found confidence ran screaming in the other direction. My drama teacher, a kindhearted man, did his best to look out for me at lunchtime, occasionally coming over to the table and shouting at people. But a frail, theater-loving intellectual yelling at a bunch of jocks is seldom effective. The food continued to fly.

I spent half my lunch period hiding in the bathroom, trying to scrub my soiled clothes (a task that is infinitely harder when you are trying to appear nonchalant in front of a bunch of popular senior girls reapplying lip gloss). As I soaked my uniform in institutional hand soap, I couldn't help but think that my Maureen friends were a little weak in the "got my back" department. Was I doomed to spend the rest of my lunches seeking refuge in the cafeteria bathroom while my friends chatted away at the table, enjoying their food instead of wearing it? My mind started to wander. *Maybe I should try to make friends with the shy Chinese exchange student whose red Keds I see peeking out beneath the stall every day? Chai Chow must be lonely; why else does she hide in a bathroom stall? I'll bet Chai Chow would stand up for me. She survived Communist China. What was a burrito to the head compared with Tiananmen Square?* When Chai Chow finally emerged from her stall to wash her hands, she looked at me cleaning my clothes at the sink like I was a hobo bathing in the river. Frightened of me, she ran away.

My mom had started questioning me as to why my uniform was always so stained at the end of the day. At first I tried to play down what was going on. But like an abused wife who can't cover up her black eye, I couldn't hide the pepperoni grease that stained my polo shirt. Eventually I told my mom the truth. She was too smart to hide anything from, and her questioning was becoming more intimidating.

"What the hell is going on, Lizzie? You don't even eat pepperoni, so don't bullshit me; I want the truth." So I told her. Just as I had suspected, she was furious. "Don't they have lunch monitors at this school? What do these people do, stand around and pick their nose while my daughter gets battered?! What a bunch of morons!" When I told her the kid who was behind it, she started railing about how he was the shortest person she had ever seen who wasn't actually a dwarf and mumbled something about him probably having tiny balls. "This little shit isn't going to take his Napoleon complex out on my kid!"

In the middle of my explanation to my mother, my brother Frank came by the house to check his mail. When he heard what was going on, he went through the roof. Suddenly my oldest brother, a highly respected college professor revered for his deep religious and moral convictions, was tearing through the phone book feverishly trying to find Chad Pratt's number while grunting things like, "I'm going to rip his balls off!" (tiny ones, according to my mother's estimation). This is the way my family operates: one of us is in trouble, and the rest of the family rallies around ready to destroy their opponent. By the time my dad got home from work, my victimization was the story of the day. My father started making plans to go down to the school. This is where I tried to put a stop to the Beckwith war machine. My brother ripping off Chad Pratt's balls was one thing, but my parents coming down to the school and yelling at people? Please God, no. That would be over the top.

After a lot of pleading, my parents assured me that they would not come down to the school. They lied. The next afternoon, a smirking Chad Pratt taunted me with the information, "You sent your parents here to protect you!" It was obvious by the shit-eating grin on his face that my parents had not been allowed to confront him themselves. If they had, he would not be smiling. They would have destroyed him through psychological torture and the threat of physical harm. Now I was pissed. I mean sure, I didn't want my parents to come down to the school because of the potential humiliation, but if they were going to come, they better damn well be permitted to ruin this kid.

My parents were pissed, too. I was their fourth and final child matriculating through BGHS, and my mom and dad had a good relationship with the school. So when my father pointed his finger in the face of the vice principal and demanded, "Bring him in here!" they were shocked that this was against policy. "Bullshit! You mean to tell me you're gonna protect the bully?! Meanwhile my daughter's scared to go to lunch and her clothes are ruined! I want to see this kid, I've got a few things to say!"

Much as I didn't want any familial assistance, my adolescent mind couldn't help but fantasize about a twisted, surreal *Goodfellas*-like scenario in which my three brothers—the professor, the optometrist, and the algebra teacher— jump out of the vice principal's closet wearing matching jogging suits and kick the living crap out of a terrified Chad Pratt.

Even though my parents were not given the privilege of

a face-to-face with Chad, their visit was effective. As if by magic, every day our lunch table was suddenly patrolled by any one of a number of different faculty members. Eventually the food stopped flying altogether, although the threats remained and I could never really relax at lunch the rest of that year. To this day, if a food fight breaks out my entire body tenses up and my eyes dart around looking for the nearest exit.

I should also mention that after a yearlong boycott, Bonnie and I became best friends again. Although she had been absent during the dark chapter of refried beans in my hair, somehow it was like we picked up right where we had left off before all the teenaged weirdness got in the way. We were back to our old selves again, and it was a huge relief. I had really missed her. Now at least I knew that if anyone threw a four-hundred-degree burrito at my head, Bonnie would be by my side yelling at them and threatening to "sue you, you stupid fucker!" And even if she wasn't, I knew my family would be there, prepared to rip off tiny balls if they had to.

Discussion Questions

1. Should Elizabeth's parents have been honest about their plans to go down to the school?
2. How might things have been different had Mr. Beckwith been given the opportunity to have a face-to-face with Chad Pratt?
3. Do you feel like throwing food at Elizabeth right now?

> ## Homework!
> Go to your local park and study the children.* Have fun trying to pick out the Bullies, Queen Bees, and Demon Children from the pack.

Oh boy, I was just about to summarize this chapter when the mailman arrived. Looks like I've ruffled a few feathers. I'd better deal with this.

Dear Elizabeth,

  I am so offended by the repeated references to children as "demons," "monsters," and "bitches." I think you are the monster.

Signed,
Appalled

Dear Appalled,

  I apologize. I hope you know that I love children. I respect children. Please understand that I would never use a negative or cruel word to describe a child (at least, not in front of their bitchy, satanic faces. Ha! See what I did there? No? Still not a fan? Sorry).

With sincerest regret,
Elizabeth Beckwith

---

* If you are a man, you'll need to be extra careful not to appear to be a pervert. Please don't wear a trench coat.

Elizabeth,

> *Hey, Chad Pratt here. I just read your essay recollecting our high school days, and I was instantly filled with shame. Wow, I was such a tool! I am so embarrassed for myself. Please accept my sincerest apologies.*
>
> *Chad Pratt*

P.S. Your mom was right, I have tiny balls.

Dear Chad,

> As far as I am concerned, it takes big balls to apologize so sincerely. Thank you. Apology accepted.
>
> EB

The Wisdom of My Father

The following is an excerpt from my brother Jim's tribute to my father at his seventy-fifth birthday party roast. Jim had just finished recounting the story of when he and my brother Frank were fifteen and sixteen years old and Mr. Teen Olympia, Glen Knoll, and his bodybuilder buddies ran them off the road, chasing them by car through the neighborhood. It is a wonderful example of a man dismissing the well-being of the bully as he provides paternal reassurance for his own children.

. . . I don't know how we escaped, but we made it home. As we walked though the door, our hearts were racing and our palms sweating. We told our dad the whole story and then he said the perfect

things to us. "Well, boys, in this life, there is always gonna be someone bigger and stronger than you, no matter who you are, and that goes for Glen Knoll too." Now, had Ward Cleaver been talking to Wally and the Beav, he would have stopped there. But Dad went on. He said, "In fact, I know a guy who, for a thousand dollars, will make Glen Knoll disappear." Not only did we learn a valuable lesson that night, but we slept real well, knowing that Tony the Ant was on speed dial.

Jim Beckwith
May 2005

Summary

Look, childhood and adolescence can be a rocky road, and I'm not suggesting you go around micromanaging every altercation between your children and the jerks who make them cry. All of the pain and ridicule can definitely be character building. But if you are *right there*, your kids are most likely looking to you to protect them—if not physically, then emotionally—so don't be afraid to have a little fun at the other child's expense by working your magic.* Your children will think you are the greatest human being ever, which is key for almost all of the other steps in this book to be successful. Trust me, it will be much easier to manipulate your kids if they worship you, *and* you will make them feel better.

---

* It is not really accurate to say "at their expense" since you will actually be doing them and their parents a giant favor. Some people will call playing mind games with other people's children "unethical"; I call it a "win-win."

5

Don't Be Afraid to Raise a Nerd

"They'd better just get the kid a computer and turn her into a nerd."

—My mother commenting on a five-year-old girl who had an overenthusiastic interest in boys

Before we begin, let me just make it clear that when I speak of nerds, I am not referring to the pocket protector–wearing, bow tie–clad characters from eighties movies. I don't really see too many kids like that in the real world, although when I do, I think they are pretty fantastic. I am merely speaking of kids whose odd interests, mannerisms, and/or obsessive academic qualities keep them slightly out of touch with the mainstream, thereby denying them a ticket to the popular table.

A lot of parents, still caught up in the rat race of popularity that dominated their bygone youth, see in their children a chance to "get it right." Many of these adults are more obsessed with their children's social ranking than the children themselves. They think that if their kids run with the popular crowd, they will have a happier life and a brighter future. I'm not so sure.

Why the obsession with popularity? Do you want your teenager to be rolling around naked in the back of a car, surrounded by empty beer cans? Studies have shown that the more popular a child is, the earlier he or she experiments with sex and alcohol. Okay, maybe not actual "studies," but in my half-assed observations,* this seems to be the case. Don't worry if your son is a sophomore in high school, does not excel in sports, and has yet to hit the five-foot mark. This can only delay sexual activity and force him to develop a sharp sense of humor to deflect the ridicule he will most likely face. Then when he finally hits a growth spurt, he'll be funny *and* tall. Even if he never really becomes "tall," who cares? Did you really think your son was going to be the next Wilt Chamberlain?†

Don't be in such a hurry to wax your daughter's eyebrows and give her a makeover to help her out of her awkward stage. I say let her be awkward for as long as possible. Being hot at fourteen is a recipe for disaster; it is much safer to have a unibrow and chapped lips. I am not saying you should encourage your children to be hideous and unpopular. You want them to have healthy amounts of self-esteem and friends, just not unhealthy friends with too much self-esteem.

---

* Although my observations are half-assed, I am surprisingly dead-on most of the time (at least in my half-assed observations, I am).

† Admittedly, not exactly the most modern reference, but "the next Lew Alcindor" was already taken.

You want your kids to feel good about who they are and how they look, but with just enough of an oddball quality to keep them in the B group and out of trouble. There are typically several different enclaves of B groups, consisting of various combinations of smart kids, drama kids, comic book geeks, and female basketball players. They have a healthy mix of friends, but they sit in a different area of the cafeteria than the "beautiful people." Not that a lot of these kids aren't physically beautiful in their own right, but they usually possess the type of beauty that is not appreciated by other adolescents, or they have yet to blossom. That is a good thing. Being a late bloomer is a gift, even though it may not feel like it for the kid waiting to bloom.

One of the many fantastic benefits of being in the B group is that you have a much better chance of developing into a unique individual. These kids take more pride in being original, be it in thoughts and ideas or in a rare fashion find that they unearthed in their grandfather's attic and can't wait to wear to school. The B group kids appreciate that which is rare. As opposed to the climbers of the A group, who claw to get what everyone else has.

Kudos to the Parents of the Following Wonderfully Offbeat Kids

- The Caucasian girl who works the counter at the take-out sushi restaurant in our neighborhood. She bows like a geisha when you enter and understands enough Japanese to know what her boss, the Japanese equivalent of Mel Sharples, is saying when he yells at her. This kid puts the *Asian* in *Caucasian*, baby.

- Thirteen-year-old Mary, my next-door neighbor, who, as I type this, is busy setting up her new sidewalk business venture: Lemonade and Cat Clothes.

- My oldest nephew, Dean, who never met a top hat he didn't like, and has been known, on occasion, to carry a briefcase to school. The image of him showing up to Advanced Calculus like an old-time doctor making house calls never ceases to delight me. Fantastic.

Help, My Kid Is Really Good Looking and Popular!

Relax. There are more than a fair share of kids in the A group who are smart and stay out of trouble. But if your kid has a natural wild streak and is running with the popular crowd, you need to nip this in the bud immediately. Believe me, that kid is just waiting for you to go out of town so that he can turn your house into Plato's Retreat.

The best way to deal with this is to catch it while the child is still very young. If your fifth-grade son has that twinkle in his eye like he is just dying to nail his teacher, you may want to buy him some elf ears and introduce him to Dungeons and Dragons. If, however, your child is already well into her teen years, it is probably too late to turn her into a nerd. The best thing for you to do in this scenario is to use the techniques we discussed in Chapter 1 (commenting on people) and Chapter 3 (fear and shame) to help them feel ashamed and in turn guilty—thus reducing the odds that they will participate in illicit activities that you frown on, such as selling fake IDs out of your garage or posting a sex tape of the aforementioned drunken orgy on the Internet. You do not want your teenager having sex at all, let alone on YouTube, with the unsettling image of your wedding portrait coming in and out of focus in the background.

Again, the best way to tackle this is to get to it early, while their little personalities and worldviews are still being shaped. You cannot control whom your child befriends, and you should not try to—at least, not on the surface. Instead, use the manipulation tools that you have been developing to send messages to your kid about some of the peers in his or her class and neighborhood. This involves the same kind of commenting that I spoke about in earlier chapters. Your daughter may still become friends with the girl with the extra-short skirt, but at least she will know that Cindy looks like a stripper as she swings herself around the pole at the playground and will think twice before fashioning herself as some kind of predator's cupcake. (Yes, it is okay to say that a ten-year-old looks like a stripper, because, let's be honest, some of them do.)

Which reminds me to make my plea: mothers, please stop sexualizing your little girls. An eight-year-old should not be "sexy." I think some of you are more frightened of your child becoming an overlooked nerd than a popular ho. You may be thinking, "I was a popular ho, and I turned out okay." No, you didn't. Now you're a forty-year-old ho. By the way, I've seen you at my gym, and those shorts look ridiculous on you.

Warning Signs That Your Daughter May Be Oversexualized

If any of the following apply to your young child, get her on the nerd track immediately.

- Asks to be a Pussycat Doll for Halloween
- Wants to work at Pink Taco when she grows up
- Customizes her school uniform to look "more like a Bratz doll"

Clearing the Air

Sometimes, before you can guide your offspring into their social niche, allowing them to form healthy relationships, you need to come to terms with your past. The following letter has been a long time coming.

An Open Letter to Jules Jenner

Dear Jules,

Hi, it's Elizabeth Beckwith here. I don't know how well you remember me, but we went to school together from kindergarten through twelfth grade. Every year you asked me if I was Lebanese, and I'd explain that no, I'm Italian. Does that ring a bell? Anyway, I'm writing because I am haunted by an incident that happened in first grade. I can't help but believe that this misunderstanding was

---

crucial in shaping our relationship (or lack thereof) for the eleven years that followed.

For my sixth birthday I had a Miss Piggy-themed party at my house. I invited THE ENTIRE CLASS. Thirty-five kids. It was a wild, fun party, and at one point I think I threatened to beat up Jason Kelley for making some crack about me. Coincidentally, the only other times I have ever threatened anyone with bodily harm were also at parties, but I was much older and very drunk. I can assure you, at my sixth birthday party I was very sober, although I may have been more than a little hopped up on rock candy. But that is neither here nor there.

The following Monday at school you approached me and asked why you hadn't been invited to my party. You (and apparently your mother) were offended that you were the only one in the class not invited to my party. What? Are you kidding me? Of course you were invited to my party! You were like ten million times more popular than I was. Not inviting you would have been like social suicide. I tried to explain that the entire class was invited and there must have been some mistake. Maybe you were absent the day I passed out the invitations? Nope. Maybe the invite fell out of your backpack? You weren't having it. You insisted that it was intentional. It was like a bad dream I couldn't wake up from.

You punished me by not inviting me to your slumber party the following month. You warned me ahead of time: "All the girls in the class are invited, except you. My mom said that since you didn't invite me to yours, I don't have to invite you to mine." I INVITED YOU! How many times did I have to try and explain this to you? Wasn't it enough that your grades were better than mine, that you dominated every sport, that you were blond and non-ethnic-looking during a time when Christie Brinkley was all the rage? You win! Although I must say it was probably best that I wasn't invited to your slumber party, because at the time I still had to sleep with my parents every night. It probably wouldn't have helped my fledgling popularity if, while you were squeezing toothpaste on Amy Miller's face, I was sneaking off to your telephone to beg my mother to pick me up, or worse, trying to crawl into bed with *your* parents.

In the years that followed, you skyrocketed to popularity while I remained on the fringes. It seemed you got over the whole incident because you would occasionally offer me bits of advice like, "You would look better with straight hair" or "You should be Frida Kahlo for Halloween." But I still feel an obsessive need to clear the air. Because, the fact is, you haunt me, Jules Jenner. You haunt me.

I have a recurring nightmare that you move to Los Angeles and pursue a career in comedy. The one thing that I could do better than you, you stomp on. You breeze into town and the comedy world accepts you lovingly, heralding you as "the female Will Ferrell." Even though I know that you are a well-respected dentist/swimsuit model who lives in Ohio (I Googled you; by the way, nice spread in the "Hot Doctors '08" calendar) and that my nightmare is unlikely to come true, I can't help but believe that my subconscious mind is trying to tell me something.

Lastly, I would like to thank you. Had you not sought to punish me through blacklisting me from your parties in the years that followed, I might have fallen victim to the many temptations that life in the popular crowd offered. I thank you, and my mother thanks you. (Unlike your mother, who chose to encourage the punishment of an innocent child.)

So, for the final time, I apologize for the misunderstanding, but I swear, I absolutely invited you to my Miss Piggy birthday party. I need you to know this.

Yours truly,
Elizabeth Beckwith

Encouraging B Group Activities

Everyone is blessed with his or her own unique gifts and talents. I would never want you to suppress that in your children in an effort to prevent them from being too popular. But there may be alternative activities that your children can participate in that would use their skills just as effectively without risking that they get too involved with the beautiful people. Again, your children may not be at risk for using their excessive popularity to partake in sex, debauchery, and so on. But if your kid has a natural wild streak, I would strongly suggest steering him or her in the direction of the B group. Here are some A group activities with some B group alternatives, as well as some manipulative things you can say to help aid the transition.

A Group Activity	B Group Alternative	Helpful Comment
Cheerleader	Flag girl or pep squad	"I think the flag girl uniforms are cuter than the cheerleader uniforms. The turtleneck and vest look kind of sexy together, don't you think?"
Captain of the football team	Captain of the bowling team	"Let me tell you, those guys on the bowling team are some of the most talented kids in the school. Plus they get to hang out with girls at practice. How sweet is that?"
Horny "playa" in a garage band	French horn player in the school band	"You should really think about joining the band at school. Did you know the guy from Nine Inch Nails got his start in the marching band?"

Remember, this step is not necessary for every child. If your son is a gifted football player and an all-around good kid, it would be a shame to squander that athleticism on the bowling squad, especially since there are not a lot of scholarship dollars available for NCAA bowling. But if your kid has a shit-eating grin on his face and his only goal in life is to get laid, then you are going to have to do everything you can to delay achievement of that goal, even if it means losing out on scholarship money.

Tips for Indoctrinating Your Young Child Into Nerddom

- Decorate her room with a poster of the periodic table of elements
- Subscribe to *Popular Science*
- Encourage him to learn Klingon

UP CLOSE AND PERSONAL
Elizabeth Vs. the Ellen Roberts Academy

As a child, I felt certain that there must be some secret about me that only my parents knew and that one day when I was old enough to handle it, they would reveal this mystery to me. "Elizabeth, sit down; your mother and I have something very important to tell you. As an infant you were struck by lightning, and that's why you're the only one in your class who roots for the Jets."

A lot of kids feel like they don't fit in, but I don't know how many create such elaborate backstories for themselves. Maybe I was part robot, or superhero, or the product of some secret government testing; we did live in Nevada, after all. Just how far away was our house from the nuclear test site?

Could some atomic chemicals have seeped into my Lucky Charms, rendering me permanently out of touch with my classmates?

All I knew was that I couldn't relate to the other kids in my class. It started with small things. Like in the second grade, when we had to make collages of our favorite things for art class. The other students haphazardly glued a bunch of lame pictures of toys and modern bands, like Twisted Sister, onto pieces of construction paper. They didn't even have the decency to cover every inch of the paper. I mean, didn't everyone know that a real collage should have no white in it? I painstakingly made sure that not one millimeter of my construction paper was exposed as I pasted overlapping photographs of Liza Minnelli and Bernadette Peters across a giant image of the New York City skyline. To this I added my mother's high school prom picture, some rhinestones, and the playbill from *42nd Street*. When it was finished, it looked like a sixty-five-year-old gay man had made it. In other words, it was perfect.

In the seventh grade, my best friend, Bonnie, and I would take simple homework assignments and turn them into opportunities for performance art. "Instead of writing a poem about intolerance, could we write a song and act it out for the class?" we would plead with our teacher (who was always accommodating, no doubt to fulfill her own curiosity of what this freak show might entail). The next thing you know, I was dressed as a blind, homeless person, complete with a tin cup, and Bonnie was dressed as a misunderstood punk rocker. Our own prerecorded song blasted in the background as we acted out the pain of being "different." I probably should have just dressed as myself.

Because of my paranoia about being an oddball, from the earliest age I felt an obligation to stand up for others. This always backfired on me. Like in the third grade, when the biggest nerd in the class was being picked on. I stood up and, thinking I was the first person to make this argument, said to the bully, "Hey, how would you like it if somebody said those things to you?"

To which the bully replied, "If you love him so much, why don't you marry him?"

Ouch. Standing up for the nerd was one thing, but marriage? No thanks. I made one last attempt to reason with the bully, explaining to him why his logic was flawed. "Just because I am not willing to marry Lewis does not mean that I have no right to defend him when you call him a gaywad." One of the benefits of having a philosophy scholar as a brother was being able to recognize *reductio ad absurdum* as an eight-year-old.

He countered my argument by firing a spitwad into my eye. I guess no one in the bully's family majored in philosophy.

The injustice that pained me the most during my elementary school years was an annual basketball game that our school hosted against a place that I'll call the Ellen Roberts Academy. Ellen Roberts was a school for the mentally challenged. Sitting among my peers as they giggled at the Ellen Roberts kids was more than I could handle. In fairness, the Ellen Roberts Academy players weren't really kids at all. Most of them were gigantic and appeared to be in their early to midtwenties.* I also didn't appreciate the way it seemed like our team wasn't trying their hardest, as though their opponents weren't equals. I could think of at least three kids on our team who I was certain were more challenged mentally than the actual mentally challenged kids. I thought to myself, *One day I will play in this game, and I will play my hardest, because these people deserve respect!*

My opportunity finally came. At last, as a sixth-grader and a member of the girls' basketball team, I was eligible to play in the big co-ed Ellen Roberts Academy game. I was ecstatic. Finally, a chance to show people what good sportsmanship and human decency were all about. I laced up my Air Jordans and began my highly structured stretching routine.

My enthusiasm for the game of basketball far exceeded my abilities on the court. Offensively, I was less than stellar, but I was a fiery, relentless defender. I may not have been blessed with speed or tremendous leaping ability, but I had a secret weapon: arms that were much longer than necessary for my body. I used these arms to either steal the ball or get into a jump-ball situation with my opponent that often resulted in a turnover for my team.

Now I was prepared to work my magic against the Ellen Roberts Academy Turtles. We won the tip-off. The ball was tipped to Trevor James, a cute eighth-grade point guard who I was secretly hoping to impress with my knowledge of the game. As Trevor and I made our way down the court, I whispered to him, "I'll set a pick . . . open up the lane for you."

---

* They probably were not that old, but when you are a little kid, anybody over five-nine seems ancient.

He gave me a confused look, a look that suggested he had never seen me before in his life. He looked down at my jersey and back at my face like he was trying to figure out if I was actually on the team. It was during this awkward exchange that one of the Turtles seized the moment, stealing the ball from Trevor and scoring the first two points of the game with a violent layup.

I felt personally responsible for the stolen ball and the subsequent bucket that followed, and I was prepared to make up for it. Since I was the one bringing the ball up the court, I figured, instead of rotating the ball around the key and placing it in a more capable player's hands, why not take it all the way to the hole myself? The answer to that should have been, "Because your layup percentage is fifty percent and there is a three-hundred-pound man-boy in tiny shorts standing between you and the basket." But, feeling invincible, I went for it. Making my way to the hoop with awkward determination, I proceeded to get called for charging as I slammed into my gigantic opponent, bouncing right off him as though his chest had been a trampoline.

Shaking it off, I picked myself up off the floor and ran back to the other end of the court to set up for defense. I reminded myself that defense was my specialty; I believed in my heart that this was where I could make an impact.

The same kid who I had just slammed into was my "man" on defense. When the ball finally came his way, I made my move. I got down low and used my spider arms to make a grab for the ball. I got my hands on it, but he held on tightly and we got into the usual jump-ball situation that I had been in countless times before. It took what felt like an eternity for the referee to blow his whistle. In the meantime, we both held a death grip on the ball, but my gargantuan challenger was much stronger than I was, and the next thing I knew, my feet had left the ground. The whistle finally blew and my opponent released the basketball. I, however, continued to cling to the ball for dear life. The momentum of these two simultaneous acts, combined with the vast discrepancy in our size, was enough to send me flying across the court.

It felt like time slowed down. Everything suddenly in slow motion, I soared to the other end of the gymnasium, still holding the ball, of course. As I sailed over the exaggerated, laughing faces of my classmates, I began to ask myself some tough questions. *Is it time to abandon the dream of becoming the first woman to play in the NBA? Should I take comfort in the fact that I am giving people something legitimate to laugh at? Does this take the pressure off the kid whose balls are bursting out of his shorts?*

Boom. I didn't have time to answer my own questions before I landed in a heap on the floor. Moments later, the large hand of my "man" reached down to help me up. As he helped me off the court, everyone cheered. I was not sure if they were cheering for me, or him, or both of us, but either way, it felt good. I finally let go of the ball and smiled, knowing that the three-hundred-pound Turtle and I had touched people.

As the crowd roared, he lifted me off the floor in a sweaty embrace and said, "Sorry the guys on my team were making fun of you." It was only then that I noticed the kid with the bursting balls laughing and pointing at me.

Discussion Questions

1. How did being an oddball on the fringe help Elizabeth?
2. Do you think Elizabeth was really as "different" as she felt, or did she blow it out of proportion because of a deep-rooted, narcissistic need to believe that she is unique?
3. Are you tired of Elizabeth referring to herself in the third person in these discussion questions? If so, then Elizabeth apologizes. Elizabeth did not mean to annoy you.

Oh boy. Look what my carrier pigeon just flew in with. I'd better take a moment to read and respond.

> *Dear Elizabeth,*
>
> *First of all, yes, the third-person questions are on my nerves, but that is not why I am writing. Are you kidding me? Do you really think that being a "nerd" is going to stop a kid from having sex? Let me tell you, I was part of a nerd clique and our weekends were often filled with all-night sexcapades. Yes, we might have been wearing Spock ears and sticking light sabers in each other's orifices, but we were still having sex. I think you are a bit naïve.*
>
> *Sincerely,*
> *George K.*

Dear George,

Wow, light sabers and Spock ears? I thought most of you nerds made a clear choice between Star Trek or Star Wars. I guess you swing both ways. I can't help but believe that you are the exception and not the rule (I mean about the sexcapades, not the Vulcan/Jedi combo). I don't doubt that lots of kids from a variety of social rankings experiment with sex, but I think that in most cases, being in a nerd clique or B group delays this.

Elizabeth

P.S. Thank you for the photograph of you in a Vader mask performing erotic asphyxiation, but I do not feel it is appropriate to include it in this book.

Summary

If you are one of the many people who project your own fascination with social status onto your progeny, then it is time to stop and reexamine your goals for your offspring. There is nothing wrong with having children who are not the most popular kids in school. In fact, I encourage it. Instead of being cranky that your son didn't make the football team, breathe a sigh of relief that he is now less likely to be involved in an ill-conceived gang-bang.

6

Mind Control:
Why It's a Good Thing

Mind control gets a bad rap. The stupid Nazis had to go and ruin it for everybody. Mind control gets a bad rap. If used correctly, mind control can make a difference in your child's life. Mind control gets a bad rap.

I know what you're thinking: *Mind control gets a bad rap.* How do I know this? Because I just controlled your mind! Spooky, isn't it?

Unlike many cults and political organizations that use abusive techniques and/or psychological torture to coerce members into thinking and behaving a certain way, we at the Guilt and Manipulation Institute* use only positive techniques to control the minds of others. When I use the term *mind control*, I am referring to the act of persuading someone to think or behave in a certain way through repetitive information and by carefully controlling his or her environment.

Let us begin by looking at some techniques for creating an environment where guilt and manipulation can grow freely and be at their peak of effectiveness.

---

* Is it too late in the book to casually mention my institute?

Environment

- **Food**—Having good food in your house is a must. If you do not know how to cook, you need to turn on Food Network and take a crash course. If you really have no interest in food, then you will have to raid the prepared-meals section of your local gourmet market and disguise these as your own creations that you have slaved over (you know, sprinkle some fresh herbs or cheese on top, so that you can take ownership over the meal without having to completely lie). The key is to provide your family with delicious, homemade meals and snacks (or at the very least "seemingly homemade") that they are convinced they cannot get anywhere else. One of the best times to comment on the bad behavior of others is while your children are gorging themselves on your tantalizing creations. They are more likely to find themselves agreeing with your theories if they are mopping up your homemade sauce with hot, crusty bread while you are talking. Good food relaxes people, putting them under a spell and making them more susceptible to coercion. Plus, they are less likely to want to be far from home too often or for too long out of fear that they may miss one of your meals. Sometimes a simple "That's too bad, I'm making your favorite chicken" will prevent your child from going out on a night when you'd rather they stay home. Mary Poppins suggested a spoonful of sugar to help the medicine go down; I am suggesting a lifetime of delicious treats to aid in the absorption of guilt. The Appendix, "Recipes to Keep Your Children From Running Away," is designed to help those of you who don't know where to begin.

- **Shelter**—Unlike traditional mind control techniques, where the goal is to make your subjects uncomfortable and tired so that they will "break down" and be open to suggestion, we at the Guilt and Manipulation Institute[*] take a different approach. We believe it is important to make your surroundings as comfortable as possible. Cozy beds. Comfy pillows. Good smells. "There's no place like home" is not just a cute saying; it is a powerful manipulation tool. There should be no place quite like home for your family. At the end of a tough day at school, your kids should know that they are returning to a warm, safe place. If your son needs to cry into his pillow because someone called him fat, make sure it is a soft one with a freshly laundered pillowcase. This way, he is more likely to fall into a deep, relaxing sleep following his meltdown (reinforcing the notion that there's no place like home) instead of bolting out the door to smoke weed behind the garage like the kid up the street.

- **Tasks**—You have to be careful when it comes to the distribution of chores. You want your children to feel like they are helpful members of the group, but you

---

[*] Am I getting too carried away with this institute business? Oh, that reminds me, if you would like to be a test subject for our team of scientists, please go to our website, www.guiltandmanipulation.com, and sign up now.

do not want them doing so much that you have nothing to dangle over their heads. When my Uncle Stevie used to tell my grandma that he was going to run away from home, she would say, "Go ahead! Who's going to wash your underwear?" He never ran away. Let them do enough so that they can understand what a pain in the ass chores are. You want your children to appreciate all of your hard work, so give them a taste of it, but not in such a structured fashion that they resent you and the chores. The idea is for them to feel guilty when they see their friends sweating it out to complete their insane chore charts in a timely manner. You want them to come home from a sleepover thinking, *My parents are saints. Maybe I should pitch in more around here.* Your kids should definitely be helping out, but be casual about it. "Wanna give me a hand emptying the dishwasher, honey?" Sprinkle your requests with a term of endearment, and your children would have to be real assholes to deny you (if they are assholes, you clearly have not been following the advice offered in this tome). Let them help with tasks like dusting, setting the table, or vacuuming, but don't be in such a hurry to teach them to do their own laundry. You want certain tasks to remain a mystery. Sure, your children need you for reasons that go beyond washing their clothes, but kids seldom think in terms of abstract concepts. Give them concrete proof of why they need you so that, like my Uncle Stevie, they won't go too far out of fear that no one will wash their underwear.

Repetitive Information

It's a simple fact: if you repeat the same message enough times, people will start to believe it. (At least, that's what my cousin Jim has told me a thousand times.) This is what I am speaking of in earlier chapters when I recommend commenting on people. When the same sentiment is repeated over and over again in regard to people and things that you find disturbing and offensive, your offspring will begin to take these opinions to be their own. Eventually they will have no recollection of a time when they felt differently about lawyers who advertise or the lady at the gym who wears too much makeup. Bingo, your brainwashing has been a success.

The focal point of your comments does not have to be limited to people whom you run into from day to day. Turn on just about any reality show and there are probably ten examples of assholes available to point out to your children. In fact, just about any of the television shows that most parents live in fear of their children viewing are loaded with opportunities to teach. I am not suggesting you plan a family evening around the latest installment of *Real World*, but if you should catch your kid watching it, why not get in a few jabs about the sordid goings-on: "Don't they worry that their mothers are watching?"

Or, "That certainly defeats the purpose of showering. They might as well be scrubbing themselves with a loofah full of gonorrhea."

By repeating the same sentiment over and over, you will firmly establish your worldview in the eyes of your children. It is important that you make these statements in a friendly manner, with inflections that suggest that you assume they agree with you. In other words, instead of framing your comments in an accusatory way, such as, "I'd better not ever catch you in a hot tub full of naked, drunk people," you should say, "Can you believe those people? Are they disgusting or what?" This is especially effective if followed by "I'm going to the kitchen, sweetie; can I get you a cookie?"

Instead Of	How About
"You'd better not ever dress like that girl in that rap video."	"Isn't she embarrassed that her ass is hanging out of her skirt like that? I feel sorry for her; I bet no one ever told her she was pretty, so now she needs to shake her ass cheeks in front of a camera. Thank God my daughter has self-respect." Then, kissing your daughter on her head, add, "I swear, I've got the best kids."

By having pity on the offending person—"I feel sorry for her"—you send a message that you are a compassionate person. This will make you a more likable character, coming across less a rigid, judgmental jerk and more a wise soul who knows a thing or two about the world. Inserting the reason that you feel sorry for the person is important ("Nobody ever told her she was pretty"). This paints you as someone who can read people, sending a subconscious message to your children that you may know more about them than you let on. This is good. If you do this enough times, your kids will begin to suspect that you possess psychic powers that you have never told them about. This will prevent them from attempting to hide things from you, knowing that it is a lost cause. Finally, by kissing your child on the head and complimenting her, you reinforce that you assume your kid would never dress like the girl in the video, because your kid is perfect. Now if your daughter is ever tempted to dress slutty, she will feel too shitty about herself to follow through. And you did it all by telling her what a great person she is; you did it through compliments and hugs. You did it through mind control. Congratulations.

The Hypnotic Effect of Family Legends

Sitting around the table, pastry in hand, sharing funny family stories is not only a great way to bond, but also a fun, safe way to hypnotize your children. This method is twofold.

- **Full stomach + rich, buttery dessert = relaxed state**— As I mentioned earlier, your kids are more open to suggestion if they are relaxed and content, and they are more relaxed and content after a delicious meal, while stuffing their faces with pastry.*
- **Family pride**—Having legendary relatives is a great source of pride for most people. Your kids will hang on every word as you tell about the time Poppy hung your uncle out the window for hitting your aunt. In your classic retelling, you will not only reinforce that spousal abuse is sick, but you will send the subliminal message that no one can top your family when it comes to fascinating family tales. This pride will keep them loyal to

---

* Chocolate is an especially helpful mind control dessert; it has been scientifically proven to lower blood pressure, thus putting one in the relaxed state necessary for brainwashing to be at its most effective.

your value system and will have them returning to the family table for years to come.

For this method to work, not only do you need great stories, but you also need to be a great storyteller. You most likely have the stories. Every family has at least one tale of legendary status; you just may need to dig around a little bit. There may be some things that you swore you would never tell your children about that may be perfect "family legend" material. Once your kids are in their early teens, it is perfectly all right to use stories that are a little off-color. This will impress them and will keep them coming back for more, which is especially important during their teen years. Don't be afraid to pepper even the darkest stories with jokes. For example, "Uncle Johnny was such a scary S.O.B., one time he left his wallet in the hotel room after he had just been with a hooker. When he came back to get it, the four hundred dollars was still there. The wallet hadn't even been touched. As opposed to his genitals, which had been touched repeatedly."

Once you have the kids under your spell, you can weave in the moral of the story. At first glance, the moral of this example seems to be, "If you don't want a hooker to steal your money, act like you might murder them." But that is exactly why you need to continue with more legends of Uncle Johnny, sparing no detail of his early and ugly death.* It will soon become obvious that his was no kind of life. Meanwhile, your kids will be so riveted by your endless supply of

---

* Using your own real examples of course. I feel I need to clarify for the handful of people who might, in a confused state, misunderstand and use my example as their own.

anecdotes, they won't realize that they have been lulled into a highly suggestive trance.

> **TIP →** Don't forget to sprinkle these stories with the "commenting" technique that you have been working so hard to master! (For example, "This guy was a real sick son of a bitch. Did I ever tell you about the time . . . ?")

If you are not a naturally gifted storyteller, you will need to work on it. The rhythm of your storytelling is what is going to help lure your kids into a hypnotic state. Practice in the mirror if you need to, or sign up for Toastmasters if absolutely necessary.

Mind Control Vs. Behavior Control

Let us examine the difference between controlling your offspring's mind through subliminal guilt and manipulation techniques versus more overt attempts at behavior control.

OVERT SYMBOLIC CONTROL:
THE PURITY RING AND PURITY BALLS*

A purity ring has become a popular gift in our culture. It is a piece of jewelry given to a child from a parent with the promise that the child will remain "pure" until marriage. Often

---

* No pun intended.

this is accompanied by a ceremony in which the child recites a virginity pledge to his or her father and/or mother.

In a similar vein, a purity ball is a father-daughter dance in which the father pledges to be the protector of his daughter's "purity" and the daughter pledges to abstain from sex until marriage. Sadly, my side business of selling T-shirts outside these events that read *My Dad's Got Purity Balls* has not taken off.*

I am on board with wanting my children to keep their innocence intact. Not only do I want my kids to wait until they are married, I'm not even sure I want them having sex after they are married.† But I do *not* believe that the straightforward purity campaigns are the most effective way to achieve this.

Purity rings, virginity pledges, and father-daughter purity dances set the bar high. Although there is nothing wrong with shooting for the stars (the inherent creepiness of the "Daddy is going to guard my vagina until he hands it over to my husband" purity ball conceit aside), we at the Guilt and Manipulation Institute employ a different tactic. We believe that the best way to go about preserving innocence is through the assumption of innocence. In order to effectively manipulate the minds of your offspring, you must first prove that you respect your children by trusting them to make the right choices. Then, once they are comfortable, you barrage them with your subliminal campaign.

---

* T-shirts available at www.guiltandmanipulation.com.

† Please write to your representatives and encourage them to support legislation to federally fund my "Abstinence is not just for before marriage" campaign.

By creating a ceremony and fanfare around "remaining pure" and making your kid recite a virginity pledge, you are sending the message that this is something they might not do otherwise, and this is something we must cut off at the pass. Instead, the message ought to be, "Of course you are going to remain innocent and not touch your boyfriend's/girlfriend's genitals; why wouldn't you?" This may not always start out as the truth, but if this is the message that you drill into their subconscious at every opportunity, eventually it will become the truth.

If you have created your team and worked hard at your commenting, your worldview should be obvious. Your kids will have a firm understanding of the difference between right and wrong and the values your family holds dear. Add the assumption of innocence into the mix and you will have a stronger psychological hold over your children than the guy who gave his daughter a ring with two emeralds representing "his eyes always watching her." The girl with the ring may have a tough time putting her father's eyes down her boyfriend's pants, but she always has the option of removing the ring. Your kids, however, will have difficulty removing the image of your disapproving face as you drove past two teens making out in front of the high school. "How disgusting," you had said, adding your trademark "I've got the best kids. I swear."

In the following essay, pay attention to how, even as a grown woman, my mother's opinion continues to haunt me.

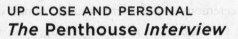

UP CLOSE AND PERSONAL
The Penthouse *Interview*

Following my second appearance on *The Late Late Show*, *Penthouse* magazine contacted my manager to inquire about interviewing me for a feature in their publication called "Stand-Up Guys." It is a section of each issue dedicated to interviewing a stand-up comic. My manager, Willie, called me to ask if I'd do it.

"I don't know . . . isn't that magazine kind of sleazy?" I asked. I had never seen an actual issue of *Penthouse* before. My paternal grandfather had a vast collection of *Playboy*, which was permanently fanned out on his coffee table during my childhood, and I had seen plenty more from using the bathroom at the homes of various friends of my husband. But *Penthouse* I'd never actually seen. My manager assured me that many well-respected comedians were interviewed by *Penthouse* and that it could be fun and good practice for me to hone my interview skills. "I know you're more conservative than I am about certain things, so I understand if you don't want to do it. But I don't think it would be a bad thing."

"What's *Penthouse* like? Is it kind of like *Playboy*?"

"Yeah, it's kind of like Playboy. Maybe slightly more risqué."

By the time I would learn what "slightly more risqué" actually involved, it would be too late. I said yes, convincing myself that it was no big deal. I thought about the long, respected tradition of comedians interviewed by *Playboy*. I was following in the footsteps of trailblazers like Lenny Bruce and George Carlin. Okay, so it wasn't actually *Playboy*. But my manager himself said that it was "kind of" like *Playboy*, so maybe in a way I was "kind of" like Carlin. I'm certain my philosopher brother would mock this lame deductive reasoning, but I persuaded myself that it was rock-solid logic. *Yeah, yeah, that sounds pretty good to me*, I thought. This was sounding more and more like a no-brainer. Of course I would do the interview. Why wouldn't I? It's not like I'd be posing naked. But in the back of my mind, it gnawed at me: "What would my mother think?" I mean, even though I would be cracking jokes with all of my clothes on, it was still in a pornographic magazine. My parents are by no means prudes, but they have a lot of pride in their children. What would they think as they flipped past page after page of waxed vaginas and glistening tits to find my comedy interview?

I flashed back to my childhood, when my mom told me about our neighbor's daughter, a young woman named Leah, who did a spread for *Playboy*. When Leah's issue came out, Leah's mother was so proud and excited; she brought it everywhere with her and showed it to everyone. It didn't matter if it was the butcher at Albertsons or the little old lady who was the parish receptionist, Leah's mom would whip out that centerfold. "My daughter is Miss April! She's in *Playboy*! *Playboy* magazine! Isn't she gorgeous?" she would gush, beaming, as she shoved the glossy image of her daughter's bush into the faces of strangers.

My mother found this appalling. "Can you imagine being proud of naked pictures of your kid? I wouldn't tell a soul!" I reminded myself that mine was not going to be a pictorial and that I was just trying to "kind of" follow in the footsteps of George Carlin, a comedian my mother herself loved. Still, I decided I wouldn't mention anything to my parents just yet.

The interview was over the phone, which was for the best, since it made it impossible for the interviewer to see the pained look on my face as he launched into a series of "sexy" questions. Why it hadn't occurred to me that a porno magazine would want to ask me about sex, I don't know. I mean, didn't Bruce and Carlin talk about highbrow topics like politics and drug culture in their interviews? I couldn't recall either of them being asked corny questions about their erogenous zones. Oh yeah, right, that was *Playboy*, scholarly porn. Maybe *Penthouse* was more different than I had anticipated.

The questions weren't even that bad, but I had worked myself into such a neurotic frenzy by seeing every question through the lens of my parents reading the finished piece out loud to each other. I felt bad for the guy interviewing me. Instead of just answering simple questions about gynecologists and one-night stands, I made a big show of how ill at ease I was with the line of questioning. I made sure with every uncomfortable sigh that my embarrassment could be felt through the phone, until I could sense that my mood had been psychically transferred onto him. The poor guy sounded like an ashamed schoolboy by the time we were through. Here was a man who was surrounded by some of the dirtiest images in the world on a daily basis, and I had somehow managed to shame him for asking me about my worst date.

By the time the interview was over, I was sweating. Didn't they know how uncomfortable talking about sex makes me? Hadn't they seen my act? I went over my answers repeatedly and tried to see them through the eyes of my family. Nothing I said was too bad, but still, I have a psychological block that sends me into a death spiral at the thought of my family seeing me in anything resembling a sexual light. I tried to shake it off. It would be several months before the issue would hit the stands. No sense panicking just yet.

To make myself feel better I called my friend Paul, a fellow comic and an expert in the pornography genre. "Do you think people will ever see this? Will anyone find out?" I asked, with the desperation of someone who needed help covering a murder.

"Nah! Nobody buys *Penthouse* anymore. *Playboy* is acceptable to have lying around your house. If people want hardcore stuff, they go online to get it. *Penthouse* is in trouble right now because it doesn't really have a niche anymore. Trust me, no one buys it."

His words calmed me, but one thing he said bothered me. "Wait, what do you mean, hard-core? I thought it was kind of like *Playboy*."

Paul started laughing. "Last time I checked, *Playboy* didn't have pictures of people screwing."

"What?!!! Shut up!" The blood drained from my face.

"Oh yeah, *Penthouse* is filthy. It almost makes *me* uncomfortable." This from a guy who had devoted a third of his act to "ass beads." Paul must have sensed the dark cloud forming over my head, because he reiterated his message. "Trust me, nobody buys it."

I calmed down and convinced myself that Paul was right. No one would see it. Two months later my phone rang; it was my friend Morris, another comic. "You're in *Penthouse*?" He sounded disgusted.

"What? No. I was interviewed by them a while ago. Is it out? How do you know about it?" I asked, getting nervous.

"Everybody was passing it around at the Comedy Underground tonight. I can't believe you're in *Penthouse*."

"Stop saying it like that! It was just an interview."

"I know, but it just doesn't seem like something you'd do."

Morris's incredulous tone was testing my nerves. Like he was so above it. This was a guy who openly had a crush on the little girl from *Party of Five*. I hung up the phone and ran to tell my husband, Pat, the issue was out.

"I'm going to the Seven-Eleven right now!" he said, with the enthusiasm of a man who had just been given permission to purchase pornography.

They keep the dirty magazines behind the counter, so Pat had to suffer the embarrassment of asking the clerk for the latest *Penthouse*. But the indignity did not end there.

"That'll be nine seventy-five."

"Nine seventy-five? For a magazine?" The man just stared at him. "Crap. I only have a five-dollar bill. Let me run out to my car real quick." At this point a line had begun to form behind Pat. He sprinted to his car and returned moments later with his ashtray full of change. He emptied the coins onto the counter as the people in the now-sizable line stared at him like he was a desperate porn junkie. Pat could sense this, so he attempted to explain. "You don't understand. My wife's in this issue."

"Sure, buddy!"

"No, no. I mean she's interviewed. She's a comedian," he said as he scrambled to catch a nickel that was about to roll off the counter.

"It's a free country, dude. Just hurry up," barked an anxious burnout holding an unappetizing banana and a six-pack of beer.

With three cents to spare, Pat completed his purchase.

"Do you want the receipt?" the clerk asked.

"Nah. Actually, come to think of it, yeah. I'm pretty sure we can write this off." Pat grabbed the receipt and fled as the line collectively rolled their eyes.

I was a bit confused after my conversation with Morris. I can't remember how he had phrased it, but he had made it sound like the person who bought it saw the magazine on the newsstand on the way to the comedy show, and purchased it knowing I was in it. How could that be? That's what I was thinking about as I waited for Pat to return from the 7–11. Then I got my answer.

I heard the garage open and close and the familiar sound of Pat running up the stairs. "Your name is on the cover; how classic is that?" Pat said, laughing.

"What?! Oh no!" I said, snatching the magazine out of his hand. There, next to a sexy European-looking woman wearing only a feathered Native American headband, were the words *STAND-UP SEXPOT ELIZABETH BECKWITH'S EROGENOUS ZONES.* "Oh shit, it sounds like I'm naked!"

Paranoid as I was about having my name on the cover of a porno rag, I can't pretend that, for a brief moment, I didn't squeal in delight that they referred to me as a sexpot. Then I went back to panicking. I tried to flip to my article as quickly as possible, but was sidetracked by how astonishingly offensive the publication is. I mean, I'm not a big fan of *Playboy* either, but at least you could argue that those photos are just beautifully shot pictures of nude women. These were pictures of sex acts, and not just from a distance. I didn't even have time to fully absorb the impact of the magazine itself before I found my interview. And then my blood ran cold.

In the center of the article was my headshot, and beneath the picture, in twenty-four-point type, was a quote of mine taken completely out of context. *"I don't have anything against Jesus. It's just that we don't hang together."* It was in reference to a joke I used to do about the difference between Catholics and nondenominational Christians, regarding how both groups love Jesus, but some non-dommers tend to think of Jesus as a buddy that hangs out with them on a daily basis. Like on jogs and stuff: "Just going for a jog with my buddy Jesus." The joke ends with me trying to swim with Jesus but getting pissed 'cause he's always like, "Look at me, I'm walking on water!" It's been a long time since I've done the bit, but I believe that Jesus and I high-five at the end. Anyway, I had told the writer about an incident when I had done the joke onstage and a guy in the audience got really mad at me. As I was recounting the exchange in the interview, I must have used that phrase.

I began sobbing. I could barely get the words out between sobs: '"I don't have anything (sob, sob) against Jesus. It's just that we don't (sob, sob) *hang* together?' It sounds like I'm just another atheist comedian. That's not who I am. I love (sob) Jesus. (sob, sob) It sounds like I'm making fun of (sob) Jesus (sob) and two pages later there's a picture of a dripping (sob) erection. I'm going to hell. (sob, sob) My family can never see this."

Pat put his arms around me and held me close. "I know

that you love Jesus." He kissed me on the head. "It's just that you don't hang together."

"Shut up! Don't make fun of me right now." I threw myself into a melodramatic heap on the couch, my signature move.

I had one month until the issue would be off the stands. Every day I crossed another date off the calendar. If I could just get through this month without my family finding out, I would be home free. During this countdown, I attempted to limit my contact with my parents as much as possible. I usually talk to my mom at least three times a week on the phone. But because my mother has extrasensory powers that render her able to know everything just by the way I say hello, I believed it was in my best interest to make myself scarce. I spoke to my parents here and there, but I tried to be brief and keep my voice at a neutral register.

I didn't want to hide this from my parents. My plan was to tell them all about it after it was no longer on the stands. I knew they would never be mad at me about it, but my family is so supportive that it would be impossible for them to *not* buy the issue. And there was no way I could stomach the thought of them seeing those disgusting images juxtaposed with my Jesus quote.

By day eight, things began to unravel. I got an e-mail from my brother Jim, saying that a buddy of his bought an issue of *Penthouse* on a business trip and was surprised to see me in it. I'm sure he was very surprised. I doubt that when he brought the magazine back to his hotel room to end his evening, he wasn't expecting to see the innocent headshot of a girl he's known since she was seven staring back at him.

I knew Jim wouldn't say anything to my parents, but I felt ashamed that even he knew. Jim and I exchanged funny e-mails about the whole thing, and it made me feel a little better.

On the evening of day fifteen, my phone rang. It was my mother. I sensed from her voice that she knew something. "So, what's been going on?" she asked with an overly innocent intonation.

I was nervous to take the bait. "Nothing much. Just, you know, the usual," I said.

"Nothing new at all?" she asked.

"Not really. Just, uh . . . I don't know . . ."

"I saw your article." She blurted it out.

Evidently my father has a friend who subscribes to *Penthouse*. His wife, Carol, called my mother, thrilled about seeing my interview. Of course, that's not how she phrased it.

"Stan's *Penthouse* came today. I was so excited to see Lizzie's picture in there."

"What?!" my mother asked, shocked.

"Her headshot, I mean. There's an interview with her."

My parents went to their neighborhood 7–11 to purchase it. My mom brought scissors and gave the clerk instructions to cut out my article and throw the rest away. So, thankfully, they didn't have to endure looking at portraits of pierced women holding their assholes* open.

"I was nervous to read it, but Dad and I were relieved; you sound like such a good girl in it. Not that we would ever

---

* Of course, this denied my father an opportunity to make the pun, "Is that an asshole or what?"

think that you wouldn't, but you know, it is *Penthouse*; we weren't sure what to expect."

And with that, after fifteen days of panic, I could finally exhale.

Discussion Questions

1. Did the fact that Elizabeth's mother was in her head help or hurt her during her interview?
2. How can you work harder to haunt your own children and drag them into a neurosis that will debilitate them in a positive way?
3. Do you think that Jesus was more upset with Elizabeth or *Penthouse*?

Summary

Mind control works, and it can work for you. By establishing an environment with good food and comfortable lodgings, you will create an atmosphere where your subliminal campaign will thrive. You can inhabit the heads of your children in a way that will be difficult if not impossible for them to ever completely free themselves from. And you will do it mostly through compliments and encouragement, your disparaging remarks reserved for others. Repetition is the key. Repetition is the key. Repetition is the key.

Disciplining with Meaning Vs. Meaningless Discipline*

The word *discipline* brings to mind a lot of different images: the time-out corner, a wooden spoon, a leather-clad woman whipping a grown man in diapers. But for me, the word *discipline* invokes the memory of my mother with her arm around me, tenderly explaining why she was so upset with me, as I loudly wept. Lest you think my mom was Carol Brady, allow me to paint a clearer portrait. You have to understand that my mother is the warmest, most generous, loving mother any kid could wish for, but, not unlike the Incredible Hulk, when she is angry, she is terrifying. That is what makes her so powerful. When the greatest woman in the world is looking at you like she wants to kill you, but chooses instead to let you live, it has a powerful effect on your psyche.

It is interesting to think of how frightened we were of

---

* Wow, this chapter title really makes it look like I know what I am talking about (*Note to self: Ask attorney about the legality of changing name to Dr. Elizabeth*).

upsetting our mom. She never did anything to physically hurt us when she was mad (save for an isolated incident involving my brother Patrick and a Hot Wheels track to the ass; honestly, he must have had it coming, because Patrick was the "golden child" and rarely got in trouble for anything). My mother did not resort to physical harm, because she didn't need to. Just watching her temper go from zero to ninety in five seconds flat was enough to scare the living crap out of anyone. Certain mothers are just blessed with that gift. All they have to do is give you a look, and you instantly stop what you are doing. My mother had several incarnations of "the look"; the most intimidating version involved biting her hand (as though she were doing everything in her power to stop herself from smacking you). This, coupled with a terse phrase spoken through the bitten hand, such as, "Cut the crap right now!" was enough to stop me in my tracks and have me begging for mercy.

My mother's fuse may have been short, but luckily, so was the length of time she would stay angry. She could be exploding one second, and then two minutes later she would be completely over it and would calmly inquire, "Would you like a sandwich, sweetie?" Moments earlier she might have been yelling and giving me a slap on the hand (yes, I have literally received a "slap on the hand"; that phrase always makes me laugh because it reminds me of being a little kid drawing on my parents' wedding portrait), but as soon as I got the message, the hugs and explanations followed.

My mother understood the true meaning of discipline: "to teach" versus the modern association of "to punish." At my baby shower, a book was passed around for all of the guests to write down pieces of advice for me. My mother wrote, "Always remember to hug your child while you are disciplining them." I have countless memories of my mother doing exactly that. Often this included the sentiment, "I only got mad because I didn't want you to hurt yourself." Hugging your children while you are explaining to them what they did wrong accomplishes three things: (1) It teaches them the error of their ways; (2) it conveys a sense of remorse for losing your cool five minutes earlier; and most important, (3) it covers them in a thick layer of guilt that renders them powerless to eff up again.

When I say "discipline with meaning," I am referring to teaching your child *why* he is not allowed to do something and explaining *why* what he did was wrong, so that he understands *why* you lost your temper and had a look on your face like you were going to kill him as you firmly removed him from the pile of glass shards, screaming, "Dammit to hell!" (or perhaps something much worse). Quite simply, you did not want him to get hurt. "Now do you understand why I didn't want you playing ball near the china cabinet? If that glass had sliced your wrist, or neck, you could have died! I only got upset because I was scared you were hurt, not because I care about the four hundred dollars' worth of dishes that you broke." By mentioning the value of the item your child broke, but framing it in a way that suggests that material things aren't as important to you as his health and safety, you will accomplish an important psychological trick: making your child feel better, yet terrible, at the same time. Once this has been established, he is highly unlikely to make the same mistake again.

Turning a Blind Eye

Although you always want to be aware of what your children are involved in, there may be times when it is best to pretend that you didn't notice something. "Turning a blind eye" is just that: the act of pretending that you did not notice or are not aware of something traditionally thought of as "bad." This is an important skill to hone. You will need to turn a blind eye in moments when your kids are doing something that you do not wish to condone, but, for various reasons, you think it is best not to interfere. There are several types of "blind eye" scenarios.

- **Your child hits another kid, but the kid had it coming**—I always tell my son, "We don't hit . . . *unless* someone is intentionally hurting you or your sister and you need to defend yourself." When she is old enough to understand, I will tell my daughter the same thing. I don't want to encourage violence, but I also don't want my kids to get pushed around and feel like they have to take it just because Mommy said "not to hit." Needless to say, if a playground bully is trying to steamroll one of my kids, and my kid pushes back, like a cop on the mob payroll, Mommy is going to look the other way.

- **Teenaged shenanigans**—The teenaged years are full of mistakes and experimentation. A lot of these mistakes are important in our development as we move from childhood into adulthood. How else are we going to learn that drinking too much *Strawberry Hill* wine leads to vomiting all over the guy you have a crush on? It is better to have your kids make most of these mistakes while they are still living under your roof than to micro-manage their social life and have them wait to make these embarrassing, often dangerous, missteps when they are hundreds of miles away at college. If you are constantly hawking them and snooping around to find out if there is going to be beer at the party (let me save you the trouble—there will be), then you are in danger of denying your children the opportunity to wrestle with the kind of tough choices that will follow them for most of their adult lives. Sometimes they will make the wrong choice, but when they do, you will be there to step in with your guidance and guilt trips. If your household is overly strict, your kids will most likely wait until they are out from under your watchful eye (away at college) to do most of their experimenting, And then they will go nuts. Believe me, the naked kid who drunkenly jumped off the roof into the frat house swimming pool was the same kid who never touched alcohol until college. I am not telling you to encourage or permit underage drinking (that would make you what is commonly referred to as a "terrible parent"); just don't be so quick to not let them go to the party because you heard there might be alcohol there. Let them grapple with the decision to drink or not to drink. If they stick their toe over the line, look the other way. If their entire leg goes over, jump in.

> **Don't Forget!**
> If you have been doing your brainwashing home-
> work, your kids will know when they screw up and
> will feel appropriately mortified that you might
> think of them as "one of those people." The shame
> created by this alone will curtail further episodes of
> this type of misbehavior.

Giving "the Look"

As I mentioned earlier, ideally, you want to be able to stop bad
behaviors just by shooting your kid a certain type of glance.
As opposed to turning a blind eye, you will deliberately turn
your suspicious eye in your child's direction.

Even after I became an adult, my mother has given me
"the look" and it was enough to send me into a tizzy to win
back her approval. One time, when my husband (who was
merely my boyfriend at the time) and I were at my parents'
house, we were lying on the couch together watching television. I was not comfortable with this setup; it felt wrong to
be horizontal in my parents' house, even if we were clothed
and watching baseball. It hadn't been my idea to watch the
Dodger game in such a pose, but I thought, *I'm an adult, big
deal, we're not doing anything wrong. I need to not be so uptight.*
And then my mother walked through the room, gave us "the
look" (the "simple" version—see below), and said, "What the
hell is this?" I wanted to die. I might as well have been naked.
She is a powerful woman.

The look can be used in three ways:

1. **Simple**—The lightest version, more suspicious than angry, designed to fill your child with shame by broadcasting the message, "I know you're up to no good." Remember, it's all in the eyes!

2. **Medium**—A slightly angrier look, which stops your children midway through their mischief. The look says, "I can see you, and you'd better cut the crap right now!" This is a very effective tool for places like church, when you are unable to use your voice to stop your kid from slamming the kneeler up and down.

3. **Full throttle**—This version goes further than merely using your eyes. Usually accompanied by biting your hand, or biting down on your lower lip so hard it appears as though you may draw blood (my brother Patrick is an expert at the lower lip bite), this look says, "So help me God, if you don't stop that right now, your ass is grass."

The beautiful thing about "the look" is that it involves no words. So if your kid gets defensive at the sight of your piercing eyes and belts out a panicked, "What?!" you can calmly reply with the classic, "I didn't say a word." Which translates to, "You tell me!"

Places Where "the Look" Comes In Handy

- Church or synagogue
- Doctor's waiting room
- Rearview mirror

One of the many benefits of the nonverbal nature of "the look" is the psychological advantage it gives you. Your child is not sure how much you have seen or exactly what you know (this is closely tied to the mind control techniques we discussed in Chapter 6). This is perfect for when your kid is about to leave the house with a friend who you are suspicious of. Just shoot your child the *simple* version of "the look," and instantly, he will be terrified that you know all about "Andy." Now if he joins Andy in his devious adventures, he will be too paranoid to enjoy the ride, and will feel awful about himself afterward—thus inhibiting future juvenile escapades.

Similarly, this look is helpful when your kid is about to walk out the door with a date. I will never forget when I was a junior in high school and a guy who my parents had never met came to pick me up. He really Eddie Haskelled it, and my mom had a look on her face like, *Is this kid full of shit or what?* Later, when I came home, she was laughing as she put into words what her eyes had spoken earlier: "Was that guy a bullshit artist or what? Let me tell you something, Lizzie, anything that guy tells you, take it and divide it by twenty-five thousand, and maybe you'll get somewhere near the truth."

Mastering the Non-Punishment

Non-punishment is when your offspring are so humiliated by what they have been caught doing that they are practically begging for punishment to lift away the suffocating feeling of guilt. But instead of issuing some sort of grounding, you let them simmer in a giant pot of guilt stew.

This technique takes a lot of nerve, and it is effective

only if you have already established your team (as discussed in Chapter 1). For this to work, it is imperative that your child respects you. But if you have done your homework and laid the groundwork, no punishment is greater than the self-loathing created by the non-punishment.

HELPFUL NON-PUNISHMENT PHRASES

- "I'm not mad at you; I'm disappointed in you."
- "Stop apologizing. Just say that you'll never do it again."
- "I think you learned your lesson by kissing the porcelain god all night."

The success of the non-punishment is heightened through the use of mockery. By allowing the entire family to join in some good-natured ribbing at the offending child's expense, you are sending the message, "If you are going to behave like a depraved moron, we will ridicule you mercilessly."

UP CLOSE AND PERSONAL
Grad Night

I will never live down the night of my high school graduation. To this very day, whenever we are at a family gathering and people start comparing stories of teenaged hijinks, I say a silent prayer that my parents won't bring up my graduation night. I cringe when, inevitably, they do, trying my best to make myself disappear. I was a vegetarian at the time and my mom loves to say, "She wouldn't eat any meat because she thought it was bad for her, but she'd have five shots of vodka. She was sooooo healthy." Then everyone laughs and looks at me like I'm an asshole, which, on that infamous evening, I was.

It was supposed to have been the best night of my life. At least, that was what I was determined to make it. It had been a rough week. My boyfriend, Oscar, had broken up with me twice since Monday. The first breakup really hurt; it came out of the blue, the result of what appeared to be hasty, hormonal decision making. It went something like this: "I'm going on a cruise with my friends and I want to be free to make out with other girls." After an apology and a brief reconciliation, he broke up with me again. This time, he was more sensitive: "After giving it some thought . . . I definitely want to be free to make out with other girls on the cruise." Can't you see why I kept coming back for more?

It was my first relationship; I didn't understand that love didn't have to involve preposterously theatrical fights, self-loathing, and constant weeping. We had gotten back together the night before graduation, but things were not looking good. I was already pissed at him again for drinking with his friends before the 10:00 a.m. ceremony. Admittedly, I have always been uptight about things like that. I mean, come on, everybody knows that getting wasted once it is dark outside is acceptable, but having a cocktail in your car at nine in the morning is disgusting.*

Anyway, I couldn't wait to pre-party with my friends before the school-sponsored party at Wet 'N Wild. I am still a little confused about the location of the party the school

---

* I put this sentence at about a seven on the sarcasm scale. It is not a hundred percent sarcasm, since I partially believe the sentiment, but I acknowledge the obvious hypocrisy of it.

hosted. Wet 'N Wild is a water park, but the party was at night and all rides were closed down. Why have a party at a water park if no one is allowed in the surf lagoon?

I arrived at the home of Jane (one of my schoolmates) around 7:00 p.m. ready to party. I hate the phrase *ready to party*, but the level of embarrassment that I feel at the mention of the phrase is appropriate for the evening that was about to unfold.

I was feeling mistakenly confident about my outfit. It was the early nineties, and I was all decked out in my sleeveless flannel shirt, denim shorts, and Doc Martens, my giant fake flower securely fastened to my black hat. I looked like some kind of Eddie Vedder/Blossom love child. My best friend, Bonnie, was already there, shot glass in hand, and I was excited to join her.

I am not sure how many shots of vodka I actually consumed, but I do know that I was sitting down the entire time. I know this because I remember thinking that I wasn't that drunk, and then I stood up to walk to the bathroom and the house turned on its side. Holy shit, I was really wasted.

My memory gets a little fuzzy here, but the next thing I knew, Bonnie and I were in the back of a Bronco crammed full of drunk girls, en route to Wet 'N Wild. The windows were down, music was blaring, and a full-fledged teenaged sing-along was taking place. In my lobotomized state, I still knew most of the words to the Beastie Boys' "Paul Revere." I don't know how we didn't get pulled over by the police; it couldn't have been more obvious that we were drunk. We might as well have been a car full of animatronic pirates, swinging jugs of moonshine out the window. If I saw us today, I would no doubt be annoyed and make a bunch of disparaging remarks to my husband about the youth of today, complete with cruel imitations. But, there I was, part of it.

We finally arrived at the party, and Bonnie and I jumped out of the back of the car like illegal immigrants after a long trip across the border. We tried our best to race to the party, but we were literally falling-down drunk. We clumsily helped each other off the asphalt and then, arm in arm, went skipping into the party. Yes. Skipping. And then we fell down again. I seem to recall becoming suddenly aware that my pants were wet. I didn't know if I had spilled alcohol on my lap or if I had pissed myself, but either way I was too drunk to be appropriately concerned. Bonnie and I helped each other off the filthy ground for the second time, laughing hysterically as I made a poor attempt to dry my wet crotch with my hat. What I did not know at the time was that my parents were watching.

Apparently, while I was pre-partying at Jane's house, my parents had gotten a call from the school. A few of the parents who had signed up to chaperone the party had canceled at the last moment, and the school wanted to know if my parents could fill in. My mom and dad didn't really want to do it, plus they had company, as our beloved neighbor, Mrs. Scott, was at our house visiting. Mrs. Scott lived across the street from us and had known me since I was born. She was a warm, wonderful woman, full of sweet Southern charm. Our families had always been very close.

My parents didn't want to leave the school hanging, so they agreed to help out, and Mrs. Scott thought it would be fun to join them and be part of "little Lizzie's graduation night," so she came too.

So, while Bonnie and I drunkenly skipped into the party, falling down several times along the way, my parents and Mrs. Scott were looking on from the rapids dock. According to my mother, the conversation went something like this:

Dad: "Liz, do you see these girls? Look at how drunk they are. How did their parents let them out of the house like that?"

Mom: "How disgusting. Wait a minute, that looks like Lizzie and Bonnie."

Dad: "No."

Mom: "Yes, it is! Look at the hat!"

Mrs. Scott: (like a Tennessee Williams heroine) "My goodness!"

They kept their distance, observing from afar.

Blissfully unaware that I was being watched, I stumbled into the bash. Soon I ran into Jason Malloy, a kid I had carpooled with since kindergarten. He appeared confused by the sight of my inebriated state. "You do realize your parents are here, right?"

Jason was a funny guy, so I assumed he was playing a joke on me.

"Ha, ha! You're soooo hilarious!" I said in a smart-ass voice, falling into him.

"I'm not kidding."

"Yeah, whatever," I said, blowing past him.

Next, it was Patrick O'Hare, another one of my elementary school classmates.

"Hey, Liz, I just saw your dad."

"Oh, okay, what, did Malloy make you say that?" I said, not even giving him a chance to respond before I limboed away.

Finally, my friend Ryan, a kid who had worked for my parents in their candy store, gave me the same information. "Hey, I didn't know your parents were gonna be here, Beckwith." The rooster crowed a third time as I once again denied that my parents were at the party.

"No, they're not! Geez, why does everybody keep saying that?"

"Because they're right over there," Ryan said, pointing.

I turned my head, and slowly, first my father and then my mother came into view. *And, wait a minute, is that . . . Mrs. Scott?* The ninety-degree Vegas night could not stop the chill from running up my spine; I was instantly covered in goose bumps. It was almost enough to sober me up. Almost. Too smashed to attempt to make sense of the situation or come up with anything resembling a plan, I attempted to proceed with my evening, keeping my distance and doing my best impression of a clearheaded person. That didn't last too long.

Moments later, I found Oscar sitting on a lounge chair, glassy-eyed and arrogant looking. He was high on hash, but, unlike me, he could actually pass for a sober person. I can't remember what the conversation was, but for the third time that week, he broke up with me. I went crazy, ripping off the gold heart pendant he had given me for Christmas and throwing it in his face. Then I threw my foot into his face, knocking him off his lawn chair. Turns out, I'm a violent drunk.

The next thing I remember, Oscar was handing me over to my father, saying, "I think you need to take her home, Mr. Beckwith." This made me see red, and I swung at him. My father restrained me.

I started screaming. "Don't listen to him, Dad! He just wants me gone so he can get on other girls!" Did I really say, "get on"? If not for my perfect teeth, I could have been mistaken for a crackhead getting arrested on *Cops*, or a lowlife on *The Jerry Springer Show* who is escorted away by security to angry jeers from the crowd. The sleeveless flannel shirt didn't help.

"You're drunk, Lizzie. You're coming home. Now," my normally fun-loving dad said, pulling me away.

"I'm gonna find Bonnie. We'd better take her home, too; she's just as bad," my mom insisted.

My mom searched fruitlessly for Bonnie. While my mother checked the ladies' room for her, Bonnie, having caught wind that the manhunt was on, crouched in a stall, hidden from view, on top of a toilet. I, on the other hand, found myself in the backseat of my parents' car, next to a shocked Mrs. Scott. I was outraged that my parents were destroying the "best night of my life." As I screamed through my tears, every expletive you could think of was flying out of my mouth. It's bad enough that my parents had to witness this revolting display, but *Mrs. Scott*? I am so ashamed.

I have a vague recollection of arriving back at our house, my loud, obscenity-laced arrival waking my tough-as-nails seventy-eight-year-old Grandma Guido, who was in town for the graduation. The hazy memory of her scurrying away in her nightgown, crossing herself furiously, as I made my entrance haunts me.

The next morning was brutal. Not because I had a terrible hangover, which I did. But because I knew that eventually I would have to get out of bed and face my parents, not to mention my grandmother. I stared at my doorknob, wondering how long I could survive without having to leave my room. *How important is urinating, really? I could probably go a couple of days without hydration, right? How long could I subsist on that Pez in my desk from three Halloweens ago?* I had a bad case of what my cousin Jimmy refers to as "the Guido guilt under the quilt."

As I lay there, trying to piece together the night, my answering machine kept clicking on with reminders. My ringer was off, and I braced myself each time I heard the familiar series of clicks followed by the foreboding beep.

"Lizzie, hey, it's Bonnie. What happened? Tell your parents I'm sorry; I know they were looking for me, but I didn't want to leave. We ended up going to Stefano's house after. There were like fifteen people in his Jacuzzi. I wish you had been there! Call me."

"Elizabeth, it's Jane. I hope you're okay, sweetie. I found a heart necklace by the Tunnel of Thunder; the chain's broken, but I think it's yours. It has your initials. Let me know."

"Hi, Liz. It's Oscar. Thanks for the black eye. Just so you know, all my friends think you are an abuser. I think it's for the best if we stay broken up."

I put the blankets over my head and tried my hardest to go back to sleep, hoping that when I woke up I would discover that it had all been a horrible dream. No such luck. I could hear my parents and Grandma shuffling around the house.

"Lizzie up yet?" my dad asked my mother. "She still sleeping it off?"

"What the hell happened last night?" my grandmother demanded. "She'd better start asking the Blessed Mother for forgiveness!" I could hear her rosary beads rattling as she spoke.

At noon, I finally made my way out of my room. My mom was on the couch, reading her novel. "Well, good morning. Can I fix you a drink?"

My dad appeared moments later and joined in the mocking. "Look what the cat dragged in! Sorry we 'fucking ruined the fucking best night of your fucking life,'" he said, mimicking me. They were really enjoying this.

Hearing my father speak my ugly words back to me really stung. Until that moment, I had no recollection of just how offensive my language had been; it was shocking to know that I had been shouting these words less than twenty-four hours earlier. "I'm so sorry. I'm so embarrassed," I said, throwing myself on the couch next to my mother, burying my head in the pillow.

"You should have seen you and Bonnie walking into that party. Talk about the blind leading the blind," my mother said, in a voice that perfectly split the difference between disapproval and mocking.

"How much did you drink last night?" my father wanted to know.

"I don't know. I kind of lost track after five shots of vodka."

My dad couldn't believe it. "Five shots of vodka? What are you, in the navy? You're lucky you didn't die. A girl your size shouldn't be drinking that much!"

"She shouldn't be drinking at all; she's seventeen years old!" And this is where my mother first made the now-classic "Oh sure, she won't eat meat but she'll have five shots of vodka" joke. Then she added, "You know, you're lucky we were there last night. I hate to think what could have happened to you if Daddy and I hadn't taken you home."

I hadn't had time to think about it, but she was right. "I know. I'm so sorry."

"Poor Grandma probably said ten rosaries for you last night. You'd better apologize to her, too."

"I will. Whatever punishment you want to give me, I deserve it. I'm a horrible person. I'm so sorry, I feel awful. I hate myself right now." I hugged my mother as tightly as I could, hoping I didn't reek too terribly of alcohol.

"You don't have to keep apologizing to me; just don't ever do it again." My mom stared at my sickly, pathetic face for a beat. " I think you probably learned your lesson."

"Don't you want to, like, take away my car or something?"

"No," she said, returning to her novel.

"I probably shouldn't be allowed to go out with my friends for a while, though, right?"

"You can if you want to. Just do me a favor—lay off the drinking," my mother said, opening the dog-eared flap of her paperback.

"You don't have to worry about that."

My mother knew she didn't have to worry about that. She knew me like a book and was fully in tune with the shame that I was feeling. I was practically begging for a formal punishment, something concrete to absolve me of my sins and lift the burden of all my guilt and remorse. But instead, my mother made me wallow in it. For a kid like me, no punishment could have been more effective.

"I think I'll wash my car later; why don't I wash yours while I'm at it?" I said, giving my parents one last chance to scream at me and rattle off a list of demands. My mom didn't budge, forcing me to do more laps in the ocean of disgrace.

"That's okay, I'm gonna be using it later to get the stuff for dinner. You want to come with me to the store?"

"Sure, Mommy," I agreed, even though I felt like I was going to vomit. "What are you making?"

"Penne with vodka sauce."

I buried my head back into the pillow.

Discussion Questions

1. Could experiences like this have helped shape Elizabeth's intolerance for sloppy, drunk people as an adult?

2. Was Elizabeth not as bad as, just as bad as, or worse than most of the people she considers assholes earlier in this book? Explain.

3. Was being ridiculed by her parents and feeling permanently ashamed of this incident enough of a punishment for Elizabeth? Do you have the courage to use "non-punishment" on your own children? Have you established your team and earned the respect of your children to the level that this would work for your family?

> **Homework!**
> We are all busy, so why not multitask by practicing your own versions of the simple, medium, and full-throttle "looks" while brushing your teeth in the morning? Don't be afraid to experiment with hand and/or lip biting; you just may be a natural!

Summary

Discipline. We at the Guilt and Manipulation Institute prefer to think of discipline as a method of teaching, rather than a style of punishment. The most effective way to manipulate your child into not repeating unsavory behavior is through loving guidance and shameful glances. By mastering the look, the blind eye, and non-punishment, you will teach your children right from wrong by giving them room to screw up, thus allowing them to experience the power of the humiliation that follows. Some kids need to do a test-drive of life as an asshole before they can confidently decide not to be one.

8

All for One and
One for All

Back in Chapter 1, as you first set out on the rewarding journey of parenting through guilt and manipulation, you studied the importance of creating a team. Now that your understanding of the basic principles of the Guilt and Manipulation philosophy has improved, and your capacity for using these methods has increased, the time has come to revisit and expand on this theme. In this chapter we will explore the importance of team activities and the critical role they play in attaining Group Think.

Group Think

First let us take a moment to define our terms. The good folks at www.answers.com define Group Think or *groupthink* as:

> *n. The act or practice of reasoning or decision-making by a group, especially when characterized by uncritical acceptance or conformity to prevailing points of view.*[*]

---

[*] www.answers.com/topic/groupthink.

As should come as no surprise, we at the Guilt and Manipulation Institute apply a slightly different meaning to the term:

n. The act or practice of loving the same things and collectively dismissing competing entities as "weak," "less than," or "bullshit."

We at the Guilt and Manipulation Institute also take issue with the idea that Group Think involves a lack of critical examination. On the contrary, we believe that critical examination is crucial in every area of one's life. But we also encourage your family to critically examine things as a team, as in, "Can you believe they have the nerve to call this pizza? This doesn't even come close to _____" (fill in the blank with the name of your favorite pizzeria). Then everyone can take turns chiming in with their comments: "This cheese has no flavor!" "The crust is like cardboard!" "Who recommended this place again? He must not know good food, poor guy." And so on.

Establishing Group Think is important for two reasons. It is fundamental to creating a comfort zone where your family (that is, your team members) always knows that they fit in, and it is critical in shaping and strengthening your psychological hold over your offspring. Let me be clear; I am not suggesting that your kids have to love everything you love. That is unrealistic and unhealthy. Originality and independent thinking are important and should always be encouraged. But ideally, there should be one or two areas (with related activities) where your family thinks as one. This is why it is imperative that you find common causes and interests to rally around as a team. The easiest and most enjoyable areas in which to achieve this are food and sports.

Food

You know that hole-in-the-wall Mexican restaurant that you discovered by accident and your family loves? What if I told you that the sheer act of dining there with your kids while mocking the food of competing establishments is one of the best bonding activities you can do with your family? I would bet you would be pretty excited by the simplicity and delicious nature of this activity. Well, guess what? That's right, it's true. So enjoy your carne asada knowing that you are giving your children a gift that goes beyond mere chips and salsa.

Having an eatery that makes your family feel superior to people not "in the know" is a great way to pass on an appreciation of good food while instilling the preferences of your team. Having something positive that makes your family feel a cut above others is a good thing. Subconsciously, your children will not want to stray from the pack for fear of being reduced to the ranking of outsiders who are not privy to the advanced tastes of your team. This need to adhere to the value system of the team will carry over into areas other than food, and that is exactly what you are striving for. Please understand, I am not encouraging you to be an uppity snob about materialistic things like cars or shoes. That would make you an asshole. I am speaking of being a snob about things that people of any social ranking can have access to—things such as pizza or sports (more on this in a moment).

Being a food snob does not mean that you eat only

expensive food; it means that you eat only *good* food. If you have a daughter, raising a family of foodies has the added benefit of diminishing the chances of her developing a dangerous eating disorder,[*] since eating will provide heightened pleasure and will be seen as a sacred event.

If you are not a natural-born foodie, you may need a little help from trusted friends. Typically, associates of a particular ethnicity are ideal to ask about which restaurants from their heritage are the best in your area. Occasionally this will backfire and someone will accuse you of reducing them to a cultural stereotype.[†] But usually people are more than happy to share their insights about the food of their culture.

THE EASIEST TYPES OF FOOD TO BECOME SNOBBY ABOUT

- Italian
- Chinese
- Mexican
- Pizza (although technically this is Italian, it has really become its own subgenre at this point, so we have given it its own category)
- Bagels

---

[*] This theory has not been formally tested, but our team of scientists is working on it. There are still five spots available in our test group. If your daughter is between ages twelve and seventeen, refuses to eat pizza from national chains, and is not currently on any medication, please visit our website to apply.

[†] This usually happens if you are too specific, as in, "Where's the best place to get chitlins?" as opposed to, "Where is the best place to get soul food?"

Just because you have a shared preference and look down on the tastes of others does not mean you have to be rude about it, starting unnecessary feuds with other families. It is fine if people outside your team have different preferences; they have their own teams, and that is as it should be. In fact, it is always fun to have good-natured ribbing with other families regarding their favorite eateries.

We had many of these types of rivalries with different friends and neighbors, but one in particular stands out in my mind. It was the week of my brother Jimmy's wedding in San Diego. It was nonstop fun as we engaged in a variety of parties and sightseeing adventures with our relatives who had traveled to Southern California for the wedding. My favorite activities involved bonding with the bride's family, with whom I instantly hit it off. As is often the case with my family, it did not take long for the conversation to turn to food.

I was only eleven years old, but I was full of opinions, so when my future sister-in-law, Kim, started talking about her family's favorite pizza place, Filipe's, I couldn't wait to jump all over her. "Kim, but you've eaten with us at New York Pizza.* You know it's the best. What are you talking about?" I said, laughing as though she had just swallowed a bottle of crazy pills.

Jim laughed. "I know, Kim and her family prefer Filipe's. I've eaten there with them. It's good, but it's no New York Pizza."

"Yeah, 'cause it's better!" Kim chimed in.

"Blasphemer!" my brother Patrick called out from two rooms away.

---

* Now known as Metro Pizza, and still the best.

It was on. It was decided that we would all dine at Filipe's and those of us who had eaten at both pizzerias would participate in a "pizza vote." Always excited to have a project, I created ballots and used Kim's father's video camera to film the entire event. This was at the beginning of the home video craze and I was obsessed with filming anything and everything, shoving the gigantic video camera into the faces of uncomfortable relatives, blinding them with the five-hundred-watt bulb attached to the top.

When we got back to Kim's parents' house I created a Larry King–style setup and proceeded to interview everyone about the pizza. I was definitely not an unbiased member of the media, throwing softball questions to my own family while grilling Kim's family with loaded questions such as, "Now, Filipe's is not actually a pizza parlor, but merely a restaurant that happens to serve pizza; am I correct?" When Kim's dog, Muffin, began to chow down on leftover Filipe's, Kim was quick to point out that even Muffin preferred Filipe's. Without missing a beat, I looked into the camera, my oversized Sally Jessy Raphael glasses dominating my face, and said, "It just goes to show you, Filipe's is for the dogs."

The pizza vote and all the hoopla surrounding it is a cherished childhood memory. Vigorously defending the honor of our favorite pizza joint as a family taught me the importance of remaining loyal to the beliefs and values of your people.

Sports

Finding a sports team to rally around as a family is a simple and fun way to create a common cause for your family. This is a method that has stood the test of time. Your children are less likely to stray than if you were to rally around a political ideology or something fleeting, like a reality show contestant. Unlike with politics, in which your kid may one day pick up a book that makes him think about things differently, there are few, if any, reasons to ever switch allegiance from a sports organization.

The earlier you can start, the better. Find a team, be it college or professional, basketball or football, and find out everything you can about them. If you can get in on the ground floor of a new franchise or a college team that has just found a new coach to ignite the program, this is ideal. If it is within your budget to acquire season tickets, get them. Attending the games of your favorite team is one of the best activities you can do as a family.

Be sure to make clear to your children through commenting that people who jump off board when a team is not doing well or jump on only when they are succeeding are "bandwagon leapers" and should be looked down on. This will send a message to your children that they must stick with their team through thick and thin, thus sticking with their family through good times and bad as well. This builds character in your children and strengthens your familial bond.

What makes this activity so special is that no matter what phases any of your kids are going through, when they set foot in that arena or ballpark, everything else goes out the window as you come together for the common cause of cheering for your team.

Let us examine how effective this can be through my real experience as a member of a family fanatical about UNLV basketball.

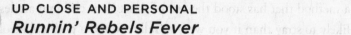

UP CLOSE AND PERSONAL
Runnin' Rebels Fever

When I was growing up in Las Vegas in the early 1980s and 1990s, it was hard not to be a fan of UNLV basketball. We had no professional sports teams in Las Vegas, so the Rebels became the primary obsession of all sports-loving people. Our family took this obsession to another level. My family had season tickets and a dog named Rebel well before my birth in 1974, and I grew up thinking that missing school to go on the road with the Runnin' Rebels was perfectly normal.

Our love for UNLV basketball brought us closer together as we cheered and wept year after year. My brother Patrick, who wouldn't be caught dead going to the movies with his little sister, would publicly high-five and even hug me during clutch moments of a Rebels game. Nothing else mattered when UNLV was playing. The fact that the head coach, Jerry Tarkanian, was hated by the NCAA powers that be only made our allegiance to the Rebels that much stronger. We felt it was "us against the world" as year after year we were unfairly ranked in the polls and denied opportunities to play high-profile teams in order to gain national respect. Tarkanian, known for chewing on a wet, folded towel during games (to keep his mouth from getting dry) was known as "Tark the Shark." At every game, my entire family proudly waved our "Tark Towels" and did the "Shark Clap" in crazed, cultlike unison, taunting our opponents along the way.

The taunting of opponents is one of my fondest child-hood memories. Shouting out, "You're sucking wind!" to tired athletes or responding to Fresno State University's chant of "FSU! FSU!" with "F-U-TOO! F-U-TOO!" warmed my eight-year-old heart. It made me feel like the sixth man on the court, like I had a purpose beyond simply being a spectator. The fact that my parents and three older brothers were even louder and more intense than I was let me know that I was part of something big, something important, and gave me something to aspire to.

Witnessing my father's superstitious rituals during every home game sent a clear message to me that the stakes were high, and that sometimes victory involved great personal sacrifice. My father wore the same outfit, right down to his scarlet underwear, to every game. I can still hear him shouting to my mother, "Dammit, Liz, where the hell are my lucky undies?" He had to purchase a program immediately on entering the arena, rolling it up in a specific way, clutching it with a death grip the entire game. On several occasions they were out of programs by the time we arrived. Those were bad moments. My father would get a look on his face of absolute disgust at the poor slob selling programs. "Ah, bullshit! You're out? The game doesn't even start for another twenty minutes! How could you be out? Unbelievable!" Then my dad would look for someone with the least-compromised-appearing program and offer to buy it off them. Then the real fun would begin.

Our seats were about five rows behind the visiting team's bench. The first four rows were reserved for the visiting fans, all of whom would grow to hate my father by the time the game was over. We all yelled and screamed, but my dad was relentless. We could be up by twenty-five points in the second half and the minute our lead dropped to twenty points my dad would yell, "Dammit, you're letting them right back in!"

The other fans would look at my father in disbelief. For my dad, no lead was secure until the final buzzer blew.

I, of course, adopted this belief for myself as I began to emulate my father, yelling at the refs for ignoring calls that I believed were a direct attempt to sabotage our more-than-comfortable lead. "Are you kidding me?! He took like ninety steps!" "This guy's living in the key!" "How is that not a foul? This guy's an animal!" Oddly, our opponent's fans did not find a nasal-voiced little girl screaming at referees very cute. They looked at our family as though our father had created a monster. But I knew I was doing the right thing. I wasn't really yelling at the refs. I was yelling at the other fans. How dare they give my dad dirty looks! *If they think he's bad, wait till they get a load of me*, I thought to myself. My heart raced; it was thrilling to get under these people's skin. I wanted to proudly scream, "I'm a Beckwith! This is what we do!"

By my sophomore year of high school, the Rebels were ranked number one preseason and looked to have their most promising season yet. The giant Rebels calendar on our kitchen wall said *The Big Year Is Here*, and it was. There were an array of unpredictable setbacks that season involving grades, injuries, and NCAA violations, but by the time March rolled around, there seemed to be no stopping us as we made our way to the Final Four in Denver, Colorado. And when I say *we*, of course I mean the Rebels and my family.

We all piled into the car and made the pilgrimage to Denver. Even my brother Jimmy's wife, Kim, made the trip. This was a big deal, considering it took her years to be allowed to even attend another regular-season game after her first inclusion resulted in a crushing loss to a Patrick Ewing–led Georgetown.

My father banned her for a while. She slowly worked her way back by attending nonthreatening games against teams like UC-Irvine and cautiously moving forward from there. It took years, but eventually my father believed the "Kim Curse" was no longer an issue. Plus, I was sure that I was good luck. This would be UNLV's third trip to the Final Four and various combinations of Beckwiths had attended all of them, but this was my first trip to the big show. We had yet to win a national championship, but I was confident that my presence would ensure the title. Clearly, I was the missing piece of the puzzle.

We settled into our hotel rooms in Denver and my father went to meet his ticket connection, Mike T., a nice man who gives off a bit of an organized-crime vibe.* When my dad returned with the tickets, he had some bad news. We were short one ticket for the semifinal game against Georgia Tech. Mike T. assured my father that if the Rebels made it to the finals, he would have enough for everyone, but for the semifinals we were shit out of luck. I had a sick feeling in my stomach. I knew I would be the sacrificial lamb. My mother, of course, volunteered to sit it out, but no one would allow that. Mind you, no one else leaped up to volunteer; everyone just sort of looked at me like I was the obvious choice. I think in their hearts, everyone knew it should have really been Kim sitting it out, but she was too new to the family to be put in that position. I didn't want to have to remind everyone who it was that took my seat for that Georgetown game several years earlier. If they wanted to risk the Kim Curse, we would

---

* Mike T. not only looks like he could have been an extra in *Casino*, he actually *was* an extra in *Casino*. He played one of the mobsters who beat Joe Pesci's character to death in the cornfield.

all pay the price, but it wouldn't be on my head! My brother Patrick assured me that if Mike T. was short a ticket for the finals, he would sit it out and I would definitely have a seat. I took his word for it, but looking back I'm pretty sure he would have tried to weasel out of that deal. I didn't say much, just sort of nodded my head, knowing that my martyrdom would not go unrecognized and getting off on the power of it. My dad felt so guilty he gave me money to do some shopping before the game. Jimmy and Patrick hugged me like you would hug someone who just lost their mother, and slipped some cash into my hand too.

I returned to the empty hotel room a couple of hours later with bags full of Final Four merchandise. I immediately put on my new, commemorative Final Four shorts and matching T-shirt and got myself a four-dollar Coke from the minibar. My mother, who was also consumed with guilt, had given me carte blanche for minibar snacks. *I could get used to being a martyr*, I thought to myself as I opened my Cool Ranch Doritos and turned on the television to hear the familiar sound of CBS Sports commentator Brent Musberger. He was blubbering on about Georgia Tech's "Lethal Weapon III" (Dennis Scott, Brian Oliver, and Kenny Anderson), and I was instantly annoyed. I still held a grudge toward Brent for his role in an Oklahoma upset over UNLV three years earlier.*

Finally, it was tip-off. I can't remember who won the tip-

---

* Brent, if you are reading this, I have forgiven you. I don't know if you ever received my epistle, "I Will Not Stop Until I Destroy You: A Seventh-Grader's Letter to Brent Musburger," but if you did, I apologize. It was over the top, I can admit that now.

off; all I remember is that the first half was very frustrating—
the Rebels were not in their groove at all and by halftime we
were down by seven points. Shit, shit, shit! I didn't want to
get too nervous or upset; after all, the Rebels had on many
occasions been down at halftime and come back to domi-
nate the second half. This was nothing new, but still, I was
nervous. Could this be the Kim Curse returning to haunt
the Rebels? I could only imagine how my dad was handling
things at this moment. My poor mother.

When the Rebels started to make an exciting comeback
in the second half, I was sitting very erect on the couch, both
legs tucked under me, my third can of Coke clutched in my
right hand. I knew what this meant. This was clearly a lucky,
rally pose, and I must hold it for the entire second half. With
seven minutes to go, the Rebels were ahead 76–69 and I was
starting to feel the physical pain of my sacrifice. I thought of
the lessons I had learned from my superstitious father, and it
gave me the strength to keep going. By the next TV timeout
I had to pee so badly I thought my kidneys were going to
explode, but I would not compromise my rally pose.

At last the final buzzer sounded and UNLV beat Georgia
Tech 90–81. My legs numb and my bladder full, I fell over
onto a heap on the floor, spilling what remained of my Coke.
I truly believed I was the sixth man on the court that day,
and I couldn't help but feel that if we won it all, I should be
hoisted onto a ladder and allowed to cut off a piece of the net.
When I told my father my story, he was so proud I thought he
might cry. He thanked me and gave me a big hug.

Two nights later, the Rebels clinched their first national

championship, crushing the Duke Blue Devils 103–73. Mike T. came through with enough tickets for everyone, and it was easily the most exciting event I had ever been a part of. Intoxicated by victory, we never could have predicted that that magical night was the beginning of the end of UNLV basketball as we had come to know it.

The next season, even though the Rebels were even better and stronger, finishing the regular season undefeated, they lost to Duke in the semifinal game of the NCAA tourney. In other words, my entire family fell into a debilitating depression. I was not at the Final Four that year. I'm sure you must have surmised that, considering I was the proven good-luck charm. I had warned my family that my lack of presence at the game could result in an upset; nonetheless, my parents made the trip alone. I spent the weekend with Jimmy, Kim, and Kim's parents in San Diego. It was Easter weekend, the worst Easter of our lives (no offense, Kim's parents; the ham was delicious). Jim and I both had to retire to our respective rooms to sulk after the game. Jimmy was thankful to have me along for the trip since I was the only one there who could truly understand his pain. We were arguably the greatest college basketball team in history; how could we have lost? Worse still, we didn't even have our whole family in one city to wallow together.

"The agony of defeat" is just part of being loyal to a sports team that you love, and eventually we had to come to terms with it. What proved to be far more painful was the complete unraveling of the Rebels basketball program. The president of UNLV, Robert Maxson, was in a power struggle with Tarkanian, and it was no secret that Maxson wanted him gone. When photographs surfaced of three Rebels basketball players in a hot tub with Richard "The Fixer" Perry, a notorious sports fixer, Tarkanian was forced to resign. When will people learn not to be photographed in hot tubs? Nothing good ever comes from hot tub photos. Where do you think the expression "You're in hot water" comes from?

Anyway, the whole thing got ugly, and at one point Tark tried to rescind his resignation to expose the university's attempts to sabotage him. My family stood firmly behind Tarkanian, wearing our *Keep Tark, Fire Maxson* T-shirts all over town. But it was not to be. Tarkanian finished his last season in 1992, the year I graduated from high school.

Thank God I went away to school in Los Angeles and did not have to deal with a Vegas devoid of Tark and the Rebels. Technically the Rebels were still there, but they weren't the real Rebels; they weren't Tarkanian's Runnin' Rebels. My father held on to his season tickets for one last season, but the whole thing felt phony and wrong. He could barely muster the enthusiasm to yell at anyone, and he stopped caring whether they ran out of programs before he got there. The scarlet underwear finally went in the trash; if it could only speak, oh, what stories it would tell.

The university had killed UNLV basketball, and we mourned the loss as though a family member had died. As the old adage goes, it is better to have loved and lost than never to have loved at all. Rebels basketball is the only relationship in my life that I have applied that clichéd saying to. Such an attachment to a sports team is something that a lot of people cannot relate to. That is too bad. Having a love for and emotional investment in something that has absolutely nothing to do with your real life is magical. Having that obsession in common with your entire nuclear family is nirvana.

Discussion Questions

1. What kind of family values can develop from yelling negative things at strangers?
2. Should Elizabeth have risked kidney damage to secure a victory for her team? Should her family have supported this?

Homework!

Find a sports team that you can rally around as a family. Get yourselves emotionally invested by learning everything you can about the coach and players. Find out the weakest element of their biggest rival and create a chant based on this to taunt them with.*

---

* Do this at your own risk. I accept no legal responsibility for any physical harm that this may result in. Please do not attempt this at Yankee Stadium.

(From left to right) Dad, Mom, Patrick, Jimmy, Kim, and me following UNLV's 1990 national championship victory over Duke.

Spousal Indoctrination and Other Related Things

It is true that opposites attract. We often look for things in a mate that are missing from our own selves, in a subconscious effort to produce offspring who are somehow better than we are. Sure, on the surface you may have only been thinking, *That guy is so hot and dangerous riding his motorcycle*, but in a hidden part of your mind, your brain was computing the likelihood that his daredevil genes would balance out your overcautious self so that you could breed a more well-rounded, braver version of yourself. A "super you." Is it biology or narcissism that drives us to want to create super versions of ourselves? I am not equipped to answer that, but I understand what Jerry Maguire meant when he said, "You complete me."

The problem is, sometimes the very things that attracted you to a mate are the things that drive you nuts when it comes to raising your family. Suddenly, when your daredevil husband wants to take your four-year-old waterskiing, you're screaming, "Are you out of your mind?! He could die!" By the time he counters that his dad took him waterskiing as a toddler, your head is spinning.

How do you win this ideological battle and get your spouse on board the Guilt and Manipulation Express? Simple: by using guilt and manipulation itself! You can use many of the methods discussed in this book to achieve spousal indoctrination.

In Chapter 1 we discussed the importance of creating your team; that team begins with you and your spouse. It is crucial that you and your partner be on the same page with your parenting philosophy.

My mailbox has been bombarded with letters from women and men all over the world who are all set to start down the guilt and manipulation road with their families but have been getting resistance from their spouses. This is an important matter to address.

One particular letter that spoke to me was from a woman named Michelle. I will walk you through my spousal manipulation techniques as I walk Michelle through them.

Let's take a look at Michelle's first letter to me.

Dear Elizabeth,

I am loving your book and am dying to use your methods, but my husband, Fred, thinks that you are a crazy egomaniac with dangerous ideas. Help! When we were first dating we had so much in common and felt like we knew each other so well. Now, it is clear that we have very different ideas about raising our children.

Your biggest fan in the whole wide world,
Michelle

Dear Michelle,

Now that you have absorbed my methods and are
ready to roll, you need to hide my book under your
mattress and start convincing Fred that my ideas are
his own. Many of the brainwashing techniques in this
book that are designed for your children can be modi-
fied and used on your spouse. Let us start by looking
at ways you can enhance your environment for maxi-
mum indoctrination. My notes are below. Hope this
helps.

Yours truly,
Elizabeth

P.S. Thanks for being my fan; you help to fill a void
in my soul that can only be satisfied by the blind love
and adoration of strangers.

Environmental Enhancements for Maximum Spousal Indoctrination

- **Wine and dine**—Filet mignon, a glass of red wine, and
  candlelight adorn the table. Maybe you're out to dinner,
  or perhaps the kids are tucked in early or at a friend's
  house. Either way, you and your other half are enjoying a romantic meal. After he has downed about a glass
  and a half of wine and is moaning over the steak, you
  can start to make your move. Be casual and flirtatious
  as you throw your Aunt Sally under the bus for letting
  her daughter out of the house in an ensemble that even
  Mariah Carey would feel ashamed to be photographed

in. "I mean, hello, if she hadn't been so concerned with talking badly about what a ho her neighbor was, maybe her kid would wear underwear under her minidress!" Then let your spouse have his turn to mock Aunt Sally. Laugh heartily and then lock eyes with him, saying something along the lines of, "Thank God I found you. We're so on the same page."

- **Reality television**—Reality television is the crack cocaine of entertainment. It's cheap, unhealthy, and embarrassing to admit that you've partaken in it. Whereas crack is the homeless cousin of high-grade, expensive cocaine, reality shows are the highbrow documentary's sleazy grandson. But there is no denying the highly addictive nature of this modern entertainment. I have a love/hate relationship with reality television.* Mostly I just hate it, but I'd be lying if I said that I haven't been sucked into my fair share of these train wrecks. I would also be lying if I didn't acknowledge what a valuable manipulation tool it can be. I touched on this in Chapter 6, and adapting the method for use with your spouse is quite simple. Find a show that sounds intriguing. If you and your partner watch the first episode together, you will undoubtedly get hooked. Week after week you will curl up on the couch to enjoy your in-house date night/guilty pleasure, and week after week you will make fun of the parade of fools who march back and forth across the screen. While you

---

* As opposed to my hate/hate relationship with crack cocaine. Let me be firm on this, I hate/hate crack cocaine.

pass the popcorn, sip your beer, and crack your jokes, be sure to slip in some carefully placed messages about these people that relate to childrearing. They can be specific: "Bruce Jenner's problem is that he never follows through with a threat. These little girls are never gonna take him seriously." Or abstract: "Do you think Omarosa got enough hugs as a child?"

While testing this theory, the Guilt and Manipulation Institute has also stumbled on another positive effect of the reality television tactic. Because of the tendency of many of these shows to court whorish people as contestants/stars, and the fact that many of the people who fill those roles either have an IQ of sixty or behave in a piggish fashion, you will both begin to find overtly sexual people unattractive.

One time my husband was at the gym with his friend and, on seeing a scantily clad woman, commented to his buddy, "What's wrong with people? Why does that woman need to dress like that? She's ridiculous!"

His buddy looked at him oddly. "Really? That upsets you? I think it's great." My husband took a moment. "I guess you're right. What's the matter with me?"*

In a similar vein, I am repulsed by tan, shiny bodybuilders who have zero body hair. So it works both ways. These techniques are not only good for uniting you in your parenting styles; they are good for your marriage in general.

---

* I guess it's time I came clean, Pat. I kind of, sort of brainwashed you. Sorry that you had to find out this way. Don't hate me!

Seed Planting 101

If you want your spouse to start thinking like you, you have to let him believe that you are thinking like him. A good way to accomplish this is to pay homage to *his* parents when trying to sell your parenting style. "Your mom is so funny. She was telling me how she'd let you watch MTV as a kid, but she'd say things like, 'See that girl up there! See how they're objectifying her! Would you want your sister to dress like that? Would you want your mother to dance like that? Think about it!' Isn't that great? I'm gonna use that one on our kids!"

It is also a good move to use the same example twice: once when she is just drifting off to sleep, in a dream state, and a second time when she is refreshed and wide awake. When the conscious and subconscious mind of your loved one are in tune in this way, moving your agenda forward is much easier to accomplish.

If your spouse has a good relationship with his or her parents, then it is important to pay attention to anecdotes of your in-laws that fit into the Guilt and Manipulation philosophy and collect these for use at opportune moments. If your spouse has a bad relationship with his or her parents, then you need to capitalize on their pitfalls that run counter to the guilt and manipulation worldview and exploit them for all they are worth.

Training Treats!

Much like you give a dog a biscuit and tell him to sit, you can train your partner to think like you, by feeding him delicious baked goods while saying things like, "Can you believe some people are afraid to make their kids feel ashamed? I mean, what good is self-esteem if you're using it to get sex and drugs?" With his mouth full of cupcake, he will only be able to utter a barely audible "Mm-hmm" as the sweet, buttery goodness sends an affirmative signal to his brain: *Sounds right to me.*

It should be mentioned, if you are dealing with a spouse who is struggling with weight loss, you do not want the treats to feel like an attempt to sabotage her. If she feels like a fat-ass while she is eating, this will send a negative signal to her brain and the training will backfire. In this case, you can offer her something delicious but healthy (you have fewer options here, but there are things out there). It is crucial to give her a compliment as you hand her the treat, so that she feels good about herself while she is eating it. Then, when her face registers the first sign of delicious satisfaction, you can safely send your message.

Bonding Through the Mutual Dislike of Others

One of the easiest and most satisfying ways to solidify your parenting philosophy with your mate is to entertain each other with stories of run-ins you have had with other parents who are clearly not your peeps.* In addition to taking the sting out

---

* Using the phrase "not your peeps" or "not my peeps" in this point in history probably sounds like I am trying to be ironic, or that I am just a huge dork trying to sound cool. The truth is, this is a phrase I use all the time with zero sense of irony, knowing that I do not sound cool at all. If you cannot relate to this, then perhaps you are just not my peeps.

of the initial exchange with the offending party and making it laughable, it bonds you and your partner and instills the message that you do not want to be like "those" people.

Just this week Pat came home from the park with our two-and-a-half-year-old and couldn't wait to tell me a story about a dad there. Michael was on the playground climbing up a high ladder, and Pat was spotting him. Another kid a little younger than Michael had just rushed up the ladder past him. The boy's dad was standing a few yards away and called out to Pat, "What are you doing? Spotting him?"

Pat said, "Yeah, I'm not a big fan of broken necks."

The other dad puffed out his chest and said, "My kid's been doing this since he was sixteen months. No spot."

Pat smiled sarcastically and said, "I'm so happy for you guys!"

For those of you reading this who do not have children yet, you are at an advantage. You have plenty of time to build a basic worldview with your mate that, regardless of whether children are ever in the picture, will bond you forever. This doesn't mean you have to have the same opinion on every-thing. Contrary to what many believe, it does not even mean that you have to have the same political views. My parents, who have the best relationship of any couple I've ever met, disagree about politics. But they agree about something much deeper and more life-affirming: they agree on which people in the world are assholes (excluding politicians, of course). Which brings us full circle to our Chapter 1 discussion.

Here is another letter that touched me.

Dear Elizabeth,

Reading your book reminds me so much of my own upbringing. Like you, I come from a big, loud, Catholic family (we are Irish, not Italian, but I can totally relate). My wife comes from an uptight, WASPy family that keeps everything a creepy secret. The only thing our families have in common is alcoholism, and they even take all the fun out of that! How can I get through to my wife?

Tommy M.

Dear Tommy,

I hear you. I mean, what good is a drinking problem if you can't even enjoy it? I'll take a red-cheeked Irishman swinging a pint, singing songs from the homeland,* over an uptight lady in a pantsuit pouring scotch over crackling ice any day. The creepy secret thing is tough. But it is important to overcome this for the safety of your family. Unfortunately, you may have to wait for something ugly to happen before you can prove your point. But when it does, jump all over it. Unfortunately, victory is a little less sweet when it includes the sentence, "If your sister had just told us your cousin tried to diddle her when they were kids, I wouldn't have had to wait till he gave his Christmas morning 'Sex with children is only damaging because society has made it dirty' manifesto to begin keep-

---

* Ignorant stereotype or the most wonderful stereotype ever?

ing our kids away from him!" It's tough to follow something so dark with "nah-nah, nah nah-nah, I was right!" But rest assured, it will be implied. Reread Chapter 2 for help in this department.

Good luck,
EB

Tommy brings up a good point. Secrets can be very dangerous. Sure, as we discussed in Chapter 2, there are certain things that you will "sweep under the rug" for various reasons, but there should be open communication between you and your spouse regarding the darker elements of your lives. Think of you and your spouse as the Central Intelligence Agency of your home. You both know all of the secrets of both of your families, and you know which ones should be kept tight to the vest and which ones should be exposed and manipulated for the greater good of your family. Let us extrapolate this idea further.

The chief responsibility of the CIA is the collection and dissection of information, which they then use to counsel our country's leaders. In your house, you and your spouse serve as both the Central Intelligence Agency and the Executive Branch. You not only analyze the information that you collect (or have collected over the years), but you decide what to do with that information. In other words, you are frighteningly powerful. Your children will start out as private citizens whose well-being is shaped by your dual roles, but as they grow, they will take on the responsibilities of junior agents who report various findings on to you, which you will in turn employ and shape at your discretion (again for their benefit).

Let me illustrate this for you via a conversation with twelve-year-old Sue and her mom:

SUE

Oh my God, Mom! You are not going to believe it! I was peeing at lunch and I heard Jill talking about Ashley to Susie and she said, "Ashley's such a ho, she'll probably lose her virginity freshman year." And then she added, "I'm going to wait until I'm at least sixteen!"

MOM

Oh my God! How disgusting! What's the matter with these girls?

SUE

I know! If I hadn't already been peeing I would have peed myself!

The mom in this scenario now knows several important things: (1) Ashley and Jill are hos. (2) Her daughter is not on board with them. The mom needs to be careful, though, because Sue may be acting as a bit of a double agent here. Sue, on some level, is studying the nuances of her mother's response to measure just how strongly she really feels about this. The mom needs to walk a fine line between being outraged without appearing shocked. If she is too shocked, Sue may be too uncomfortable to bring her any more information. But if the mother is *too* cool, Sue may interpret this as permission to follow the path of Ashley and Jill.

Armed with this information, the mom can now send her

husband on a covert mission to plant some seeds around the house to instill the message in Sue. Perhaps a few anecdotes about a girl he went to school with who dressed too provocatively. "Of course guys were attracted to her, but guess what, no one respected that girl!" We at the Guilt and Manipulation Institute are not sexist dopes, so we would encourage you to make similar comments about the boys as well. This is a good place to play a little good cop/bad cop and have the mother chime in with, "Yeah, and what about the boys who fooled around with her and used her like a toy? No one should have respected those pigs either!" And then the mother and father can have a little tiff that both Sue and her brother will benefit from.

Relationship Building

For those of you who have not started your family yet, I will reiterate that you have a bit of an advantage here. You have the time to build a strong foundation, work on your communication skills, and learn from your mistakes before you bring children into the equation.

Your marriage is the foundation of your team. For those readers who have yet to marry but plan to make the trip down the aisle soon, the Guilt and Manipulation Institute would like to endorse Catholic Engaged Encounter.* Regardless of whether you are actually Catholic, Engaged Encounter is an intensive retreat that forces you to discuss issues with your loved one that you have probably never spoken about

---

* The Roman Catholic Church has not approved this endorsement.

in a direct way: money, how you will discipline your future children, the way his grandpa grabs your ass every time he hugs you, and other uncomfortable topics. This is the perfect opportunity to establish your parenting point of view, build a strong foundation for your future family, and delve into the psyche of your partner, discovering which issues you may need to use mind games to garner control over.

Take a moment to learn more about this experience by reading the essay that follows.

UP CLOSE AND PERSONAL
Close Encounters of the Engaged Kind

Pat and I got engaged on Catalina Island. I did not see it coming at all. I got sick on the boat ride over and spent the first hour on the island hunched over a bench sucking on saltine crackers. We couldn't check into our hotel yet, so Pat made arrangements for us to get a "couples massage," which, if you've never partaken, is just two people getting a massage in the same room. For me, the entire thing was very awkward. Pat is the type of person who feels no shame in moaning with abandon during a massage. Listening to him release his tension through barbaric sounds only made me tenser. It did not help that when his masseuse would lean over to dig in deep, her giant tits would brush against his head. She kept saying things like, "You deserve this. You work so hard." How the hell does she know how hard he works? This is ridiculous.

My masseuse was getting annoyed with me. "Just relax," she'd say, rubbing oil into my shoulders. Masseuses always get frustrated with me. I am a naturally tense person, and they take it personally if they cannot break me down. But having my boyfriend on the next table reenacting a scene from *Red Shoe Diaries* was not helping.

Feeling refreshed after his massage, Pat insisted that we go on a tandem bike ride. He had pitched the bike ride idea several times on the boat ride over while I had been dry-heaving. I was skeptical about riding a tandem bike. I am not a great cyclist to begin with, and Pat is a super athlete. I was nervous about being behind him trying to keep up with his Olympian pedaling. I was certain that such a ride would at the very least result in broken bones or, more likely, paralysis. He refused to be talked out of it. Moments later I was sporting a bike helmet as we consulted a map of the island. It was decided that we would cycle to a place called Lover's Cove.

The ride was more fun than I had anticipated and, surprisingly, did not result in any injury. When we parked our bike at Lover's Cove, I was smiling. "See, I told you, that was fun, wasn't it?" Pat said.

"Yeah, it was. You were right," I admitted.

"It's because we worked together as a team," Pat said, very coachlike.

"Yeah . . ."

"Do you want to be on my team for a long, long time?"

"Huh? What are you talking about, weirdo?"

I guess I should have been suspicious, but I was completely shocked when Pat got down on one knee and proposed to me, pulling a ring out of his backpack. I was wishing I had been wearing my contact lenses. I never imagined that at the most romantic moment of my life I would be wearing my glasses and a bike helmet. I was speechless both because of shock and the fact that my chin strap was digging into my jaw, making speech uncomfortable. Finally, I said yes, and after three years of dating, our engagement officially began.

Although the word *fiancé* made me squirm,* being engaged was an exciting and happy chapter of our lives. There were many celebratory meals, drinks, and parties, and every day a new gift arrived at my door.

We knew we were going to be married in the Catholic Church, so we arranged to meet with our local parish priest to begin our marriage preparation. Not *wedding* preparation, *marriage* preparation, because, as the Church is quick to remind you, "A wedding is a day. A marriage is a lifetime."

We were required to attend a series of meetings with our parish priest, during which we took a compatibility quiz that asked questions such as, "How comfortable will you be being naked in front of your future spouse?" (For the record, I am not even comfortable being naked alone in my bathroom. Pat, however, has no issue walking by an open window completely nude. If it were socially acceptable he would take the dog for a stroll wearing only tighty-whities and running shoes.) In addition to these meetings, the Church encourages you to attend a weekend retreat known as Engaged Encounter.

We arrived in Santa Barbara with our bags packed with the comfortable clothing suggested by the brochure. After an opening-night lecture by a priest that explained the purpose of the weekend—"to give couples planning marriage the

---

* Not due to any fear of commitment or marriage, but based on my belief that the word itself sounded awkward and pretentious coming out of my mouth. I felt like I might as well have a cigarette holder and a diamond choker on as I introduced him in a fake upper crust accent: "This is my fiancé, Patrick Wuebben, of the North County Wuebbens."

opportunity to dialogue honestly and intensively about their prospective lives together"—the couples facilitating the weekend introduced themselves.

There were two couples assigned to our weekend. The first couple had been married for forty years; they were funny and had a sweet, natural ease with one another that I found comforting. They reminded me of my own parents, and I was looking forward to learning from them. The second couple was a young couple, Dave and Christine, who had been married for three years. Watching them was like watching a comedy spoof of people in love. When Christine spoke to the group, Dave would place his hand lovingly on her back and stare, awestruck, into her eyes, and when Dave spoke, Christine returned the favor. Christine had a sweet, singsongy, whispery voice; though she was Harvard educated and very intelligent, she was also a preschool teacher and had a habit of speaking to us as if we were toddlers. I had to stop myself from raising my hand to ask to use the potty.

Every time Christine mentioned God, she would make a "thumbs-up" above her head. I'm still not sure whether this is sign language for God or just an obsessive habit of Christine's, but either way, I was fascinated by Dave and Christine. They were straight out of a Folger's Crystals commercial or an Osmond holiday special. If Donny and Marie had actually been a couple, they would be Dave and Christine. I was certain they would burst into song at any moment. Were they this positive and encouraging when they were alone in their house? What were their fights like? My Engaged Encounter journal was quickly filling up with questions such as these.

Only curtains separated the bedrooms of the women's

sleeping quarters, and I had trouble falling asleep that night, drifting in and out of fitful dreams involving Dave and Christine staring lovingly into my eyes. The next morning a chorus of hair dryers woke me at dawn.

I checked my watch on the nightstand. Six a.m. Breakfast wasn't until eight; what was with the crazy grooming? I peeked out of my curtain and saw three pretty Latina girls huddled around the community sink doing full hair and makeup routines. I thought this was supposed to be a casual weekend? Why was the one in the middle wearing platform shoes? Regretting my decision to pack minimal hair and makeup supplies and wondering what this said about me as a future spouse, I fell back asleep.

The way the days were structured, we would have lectures on specific topics such as "openness in communication" or "signs of a closed relationship," and then we would go off on our own to reflect and answer questions in our journals. After fifteen minutes, a facilitator would ring the bell and we would meet back up with our future spouse to read our answers out loud to each other.

Everybody in a romantic relationship is under the impression that they know everything about one another and that they have talked about "everything"; as evidenced by how many people ran off in tears during the "read aloud to each other" portion, this is not the case. Two of the pretty Latina girls got into fights with their fiancés; one ran to her car weeping and never returned. I felt for her; her makeup was clearly not waterproof, as her previously perfect face began to resemble a melting snowman. Adding insult to injury, the platform shoes did not allow for a very graceful exit as she lost her footing and rolled down the grassy hill toward the parking lot.

This was what made the retreat so effective. It forced us to have the tough conversations before we got married, instead of letting misunderstandings build and erupt ten years later. At first I was terrified to answer questions like, "What differences in our family traditions and backgrounds do I see potentially interfering with our relationship after we are married?" Was it too soon to take a stand that leftover birthday cake makes an acceptable breakfast? After a brief argument in which I made the point that a muffin is nothing more than an oversized cupcake devoid of frosting, launching into my Bill Cosby "Dad is great, gives us the chocolate cake" routine, we moved on to other topics.

Once I saw how easy it was to talk to Pat about these concerns, it was actually kind of fun. We were able to work out concrete plans regarding future issues, such as how to split up holidays between our families. I may have lost the cake argument, but I was able to convince him that Catholic education was the right choice for our future children and that it was imperative that we eat seafood on Christmas Eve. When the questions didn't really apply to us, we had fun trying to top each other with comical answers.

The last lecture of the weekend involved intimacy in marriage. I tend to get nervous when people talk about sex, and this was no exception. Dave and Christine gave a nice talk about natural family planning and how successful it had been for them as a means of birth control, and then the lecture took a turn for the weird. Christine spoke about bringing God into their physical relationship. She explained, "Before Dave and

I come to union together, we light a candle and say a prayer, thanking God ("thumbs-up" above her head) for allowing us to join our bodies together." I love God, but the way I looked at it, praying right before sex and inviting God into the room would be like having your parents on speakerphone while you were doing it—kind of a mood spoiler, no? I know it was not her intention, but the way Christine spoke of "allowing God to be present during intimacy" made it sound like she was encouraging a three-way with the Lord—technically a five-way if you include the Father, the Son, and the Holy Spirit.*

Anyone who might have thought that Dave and Christine abandoned their squeaky-clean image and were secretly kinky behind closed doors had just had that myth dispelled. It wasn't conceivable that one could light a candle, say a prayer of thanksgiving, and then seconds later participate in a degrading role-playing game. I guess that was the point. Sex wasn't a dirty thing to be avoided at all costs until you were wedded to another; it was a beautiful gift from God that should be avoided at all costs until you were wedded to another. What I learned that afternoon was that one shouldn't have to pretend that she is a runaway teen prostitute or a vixen from outer space in order to have a fulfilling sexual relationship with her spouse. Pretty heavy stuff.

By the time we said our final prayer at the closing mass on

---

* God, forgive me. For those of you readers hoping that I receive a punishment for this, I already have. Upon my completion of this sentence, my nine-month-old daughter, whom I am attempting to sleep-train, went on a forty-five-minute crying jag. Instant karma. God is hilarious. I love him. He can dish it out *and* he can take it. Umm, did lightning just strike or was that my imagination?

Sunday, Pat and I were exhausted and ready to return to our regular schedules. We got a lot out of the retreat and left with a deeper understanding of our vision for our life together, and more important, we left with a new set of inside jokes involving Dave and Christine. They did not touch on this at the retreat, but inside jokes are a crucial ingredient in the glue that holds a marriage together. Thank you, Pat. Thank you, Dave and Christine. Thank you, Catholic Engaged Encounter.

Discussion Questions

1. Would you rather be raised by Elizabeth and Patrick or by Dave and Christine? Why?
2. Who do you think would be more disturbed by God's presence in the room during intercourse, you and your spouse or God?
3. Do you think God waves his hands frantically, whispering, "I'm not home!" to his secretary whenever Dave and Christine light their precoital candle?

Summary

Some of you may need to employ slightly altered versions of guilt and manipulation techniques on your spouse in order to indoctrinate him to our philosophy. By using seed planting, training treats, and reality television, you can slowly begin to invade your spouse's psyche until he begins to think your ideas are his own. Always remember, you and your mate are the captains of your team. Even before you have children, you are building your foundation—hopefully, whenever possible, through hilarious hijinks. If you are engaged, you are encouraged to attend a retreat along the lines of Engaged Encounter. This will help you come to a deeper understanding of who you are as a team, and will no doubt lead to a lifetime of memories and inside jokes. Maybe you'll even be lucky enough to see a pretty girl in tears rolling down a hill.

10

Guilt Is a Two-Way Street

An oft-quoted ancient proverb says, "If you give a man a fish, you feed him for a day; if you teach a man to fish, you feed him for a lifetime." We at the Guilt and Manipulation Institute have developed a similar adage: "If you give a child guilt, you make him feel bad for a day; if you create a culture of guilt, you set in motion a multigenerational domino effect that will encourage good decision making for many generations to come." Doesn't exactly roll off the tongue,* but you get the idea.

As we near the close of this book, there is one area that I have neglected to address, something that is an important building block in the guilt and manipulation psyche: your own guilty conscience. When you become parents, guilt will haunt you from the first moments of your children's lives until they are all grown up with children of their own. There's just no getting around it. The good news is that this is natural and, in fact, helpful. You cannot build a culture of guilt in your home if you have not been suffocated by it yourself on occasion.

---

* Our syntax department is working on it.

Parental guilt is two-tiered. The bottom tier is the basic question that gnaws at us: "Am I a good parent?" The top tier of parental guilt, neuroses, stems from the struggle of wanting our children to be just like us while at the same time wanting them to be better than us. Instead of helping them evolve beyond our own shortcomings, we often cripple them with sympathy (I will give a specific example of this in "Up Close and Personal"). The knowledge of this leads to an internal tug-of-war that gives birth to heavy doses of parental guilt.

Bottom-Tier Parental Guilt: Am I a Good Parent?

A lot of issues fall under the umbrella of the bottom tier. When your children are little, it is the small things that eat away at you: one minute you are worrying that you give your son too much candy, and the next you are paranoid that you are too restrictive about sweets, fearing that this may one day backfire on you. You are haunted by the image of your child raiding the pantry of his best friend, elbow deep in a box of Lucky Charms. You may think that you are only playing mind games with yourself until the day arrives that you find a blue diamond marshmallow stuck to the bottom of his shoe. It is at that moment that you will realize you are a failure on two levels. You will weep on your bed, not because your child ate sugary cereal, but because you reduced him to hiding in the cupboard of a neighbor, shoveling magical cereal into his mouth by the fistful.

When you are a parent, it is natural to constantly feel like you are doing the wrong thing and to question every decision you make. One of the best effects of the guilt and manipulation approach is that eventually you won't think twice about these little things; as you become a master of manipulation, all of these minute issues will fall into place.

Still, the big things will always torment you, regardless of what parenting approach you use; as I stated earlier, this type of parental guilt is not only normal, but healthy.

Top-Tier Parental Guilt: Neuroses

We refer to the top tier of parental guilt simply as *neuroses* because it includes your own basic neuroses about parenting as well as the fear of passing on your "issues" to your child (and the guilt involved in actually passing them on). Most people reproduce out of a subconscious desire to create tiny, improved versions of themselves. When we begin to see signs of our own undesirable characteristics in our young ones, many of us are torn. Part of us just wants to hug them and say, "You know what, it is so awesome that you have to eat exactly forty-eight Cheerios every morning. You're so lucky you have me for a mom because I totally get it; everyone you love might die if you accidentally ingest an odd number of anything. Come here, you little cutie patootie!"

The other part of us feels depressed because we know what a grind it is to live a life with _____ (insert your own issue here). What could we have done to stop this collision of nature and nurture that allowed these traits to pop up in our child?

Again, both top-tier and bottom-tier parental guilt are natural, and the Guilt and Manipulation Institute believes that only through experiencing guilt can you build your "guilt muscle" and proceed to distribute guilt effectively.

For those of you who have rarely experienced guilt, I'll deal with you in a moment. I might not have thought to include this chapter at all had I not had a recent episode of parental guilt myself. This was the basic, bottom-tier variety.

My husband and I were on our way to an engagement party. I should have been excited for a rare night out with Pat. It is always nice to have an excuse to actually fix myself up and look like the put-together person I used to feel like before I had children. So much of my week is spent running errands with my kids and getting depressed at the sight of cute, fashionable girls, thinking, "I used to be like you. Cuter, even."* It's not that I don't care anymore, or that I've given up. It's just that most days I am sprinting to get here or there, and there is never time to do more than put on my glasses and throw my hair in a messy bun.† The dexterity involved with chasing my kids around makes my "cute jeans" a frighteningly uncomfortable option. (If I were honest with myself, I would say that the dexterity involved with just getting the cute jeans over my now-larger ass hardly seems worth the trouble. But I prefer to live the lie that the jeans are tight merely because they have just been washed.)

It is pathetic how excited I get at the sight of myself after

---

* Relax; I didn't realize it at the time, so I never got to enjoy it.

† Cliché and pathetic. But, sadly, true.

I actually put on makeup, do my hair, and put on attractive clothing. I may be alone in my bathroom, but in my mind Oprah has given me a makeover and is parading me out to an audience full of weeping family and friends. Oprah pulls me into a warm Oprah embrace, whispering encouragement into my ear, as my before and after pictures appear on the screen.

I made sure to hover in front of our home for a moment so that my neighborhood, particularly the house full of college guys next door, could get a glimpse of this version of me.* I pretended to send a text message† as I allowed them to soak in my hotness. I imagined them saying, "Holy shit, is that the lady from next door? She's so effing hot! I always suspected that she was secretly hot, but I had no idea just how smoking hot she really was until this very moment, a moment that has forever altered the course of my fantasy life."

And then one of them would add, "And so young looking! She looks younger than those loud, cheesy girls who partied with us the other night. How did I have no idea that this young, hot lady has been next door the entire time? I am in awe of her youth and hotness."

I'm pretty sure they had no idea who I was, as I was unrecognizable as the grumpy woman in track pants and smudged glasses who rushes by with her dog and children in tow, shooting them dirty looks for blasting their terrible music. But I chose to believe not only that they knew who I was, but

---

* I would say "the real me," but I'm not so sure that is accurate.

† Something I pretend to do in many awkward social situations, but have never actually done in real life.

that I had now become their new object of desire, "the secret hot lady."

My tangent of low-self-esteem-infused vanity is complete, so let me get back on point. I should have been excited to look nice and enjoy a night out with Pat, with my children already tucked into bed for the night and my mother-in-law holding down the fort. But by the time we pulled out of our driveway, I was a wreck, overcome with guilt. My two-and-a-half-year-old son, Michael, had a terrible cold, and my baby daughter, Frances, was teething. I knew they would both be waking up soon, wanting me, and I wouldn't be there. Francie would allow her grandmother to soothe her back to sleep. It was the thought of Michael, hacking up phlegm, weeping, and wanting his mommy, that made me almost burst into tears on the drive to Beverly Hills.

I had told my mother-in-law, "If he wakes up, before you even go in the room, call me. We'll come right home." To some people, that may sound extreme. *Wouldn't you want to wait and see if she can get him back down by herself first? Why come all the way home? You may not need to.* Other people would balk at me ever leaving in the first place. *You went out? But your kid sounds terrible! How could you?* These two extremes live inside my head, tormenting me, on a daily basis. It is tortuous trying to balance the part of you that still wants to have a life and knows that it is important to raise children to be independent with the part that feels like you have to be there every minute to make sure that everyone is okay. Not to mention the guilt over suspecting that the only reason I was even en route to this party was because my hair came out good. I couldn't help but wonder: had my hair come out shitty, would I have told Pat it was a bad idea to leave the kids? What kind of a vain monster was I? My head was spinning.

I clutched my cell phone during the entire party,[*] which, for us, didn't last more than forty-five minutes. My phone never rang, but I was anxious to get home just in case.

These internal battles are the seeds of parental guilt. If you are to be successful at using guilt to raise good kids, you need to have an innate understanding of the concept. For some, feeling like you are the world's worst parent and ending several nights a month in tears may be a sign that you need therapy or pills; the Guilt and Manipulation Institute believes that this means you are on the right track. If you are easily prone to episodes of guilt, chances are the philosophies in this book will come naturally to you and will be more effective. If not, you may have a little extra work cut out for you. If you fall into the latter category, don't despair; I will post some assignments to jump-start you.

---

[*] Which is especially difficult when you are double-fisting gourmet cupcakes.

Homework for the Guilt Impaired!

- Let me ask you a question: have you hugged your children enough today? Make a list of the moments when you gave your kids a physical sign of your love today. Is it more than three? I would hope to God it would be. Did you know that hugs make them smarter and more confident? It's true. You may want to think about how often you give your children hugs and physical affection. I'm just saying, you know, think about it, that's all. Could you be doing more? Probably. Is a sick feeling creeping up on you yet? If not, move on to the next assignment (you smug bastard).

- Have you convinced yourself that your kids will be happier if you are personally more fulfilled? Do you rationalize spending little time with them by saying, "I need to do this for me. If I'm happy, my kids will be happy"? Think again. The truth is, your children would rather have you depressed and sitting next to them than have you absent from dinner every night, competing in poetry slams to fulfill your artistic void. Try to calculate how many hours of quality interactive time you spend with your children a week. Is it more than five? I would hope to God it would be. Hate yourself yet? Good. You're on your way!

Although an innate understanding of guilt is important, it also has a downside, one that I am all too familiar with. Often parental guilt will hold you back from helping your kid through an important milestone. There will be times when you will relate too well to your child, and you will be crippled by the memory of yourself going through the same thing. This is one of the serious side effects of top-tier parental guilt. During these phases of your child's development, it is easy to feel too guilty to do anything but deal with the situation in the way that "little you" would have wanted. This is where I get into trouble, and it would not be fair of me not to warn you about this. The personal essay that follows illustrates this point in greater detail.

UP CLOSE AND PERSONAL
What a Nightmare—How My Own Sleep Issues Have Come Back to Haunt My Children and Me

I have always had sleep issues. Legend has it that as an infant, I could fall asleep only if my dad was rubbing my back, and if he stopped, my little hand would point to my back for more. People always laugh when my mom tells this tale, not believing that a tiny baby would point to her back in such a fashion, but my parents insist that it is true. "She was six months old and she'd go like this," my mom would say, imitating the gesture.

As a toddler, I needed my dad to lie down with me in my bed until I fell asleep. I could always sense when he was about to make his move to sneak out, and I would nudge him and whisper, "I'm not asleep yet," letting him know his shift was not yet over. I took no pleasure in this nightly torment of my father. I would lie there night after night trying to will myself to fall asleep before he tried to leave. I wanted this gift for him almost as badly as I imagined he wanted it for himself. But most nights, it just didn't happen that way.

Even once he escaped my room, the dance wasn't over. Most nights I would awaken in the wee hours, frightened that a witch, a demon, or the Incredible Hulk would appear any moment at the end of my bed. I was even terrified of good things,* like Jesus, the Virgin Mary, or an angel sent down to anoint me as a prophet. To my mind, anything would be frightening if it appeared in a dark room out of nowhere. As you might expect, these obsessive thoughts would lead me sprinting out of my bed to my parents' room, where our game of musical beds would continue. I'd crawl into bed with them, it would get too crowded, and my dad would leave and go sleep in my bed.

By the time I was four years old, my parents were desperate. At the time they had just opened an ice cream and candy shop and they were telling their business partner about my sleep problems. "Our daughter had the same thing. I'll tell you exactly what you need to do. You gotta get Santa to tell her that she's old enough to go to sleep by herself." He went on to explain that there was a guy in his neighborhood that looked exactly like Santa, and that for fifty dollars and a bottle of whiskey, everything would be taken care of.

My parents went to Santa's house, whiskey and cash in hand, and met with him. Over a glass of Courvoisier, Santa wrote down everything he needed to know about me and, of course, my sleep problem. On Christmas Eve, he showed up right on time.

---

* Some would argue that the Hulk was technically a "good" thing as well. Not when you're four years old and it's the Lou Ferrigno version.

Sitting on his lap, I remember thinking that Santa smelled different than I had expected. His beard smelled like cigarettes, while his suit gave off a musty odor that I could only attribute to the piss of a reindeer. Still, his eyes twinkled, and his nose was like a cherry, and I didn't question him when he looked me in the eye and told me that the time had come for me to go to sleep on my own. He patted my head with his white-gloved hand and handed me a candy cane as I tried my best to make sense of what was happening. Santa was playing hardball with me. It was a sobering moment; I stared at my candy cane and asked myself just how badly I wanted that Barbie Dream House.

My mother claims that the plan was successful; sure, I'd still climb into bed with them in the middle of the night, but at least I didn't insist that my father lie down with me to go to sleep. They would kiss me good night, reminding me that "Santa's watching!" as I lay there nervously with my door wide open, the hall light on, and a vaporizer for white noise. I had an elaborate, obsessive-compulsive, nightly prayer ritual (which I would have to start completely over if I made a mistake). This prayer included the urgent plea, "Please let me fall asleep quickly and without any terrible dreams." Following the prayer litany I would lay my head on the pillow, trying to ignore the sound of the soldiers marching through my pillow, toward my ear. My mother had explained to me that it was just the sound of my heartbeat amplified through the pillow, but still, the image of soldiers in tall red hats, beating drums as they marched toward me, was not comforting to my overworked little imagination.

My goal was always to fall asleep before the rest of the

family retired for the night. I liked the hum of activity of my parents and older siblings going about their evening. The normalness made me feel safe. How could anything supernatural happen if my brother was watching Letterman and biting his toenails in the family room?

The nightly sprint to my parents' bedroom went on for years. As I got older, I became more self-conscious about it. I felt too embarrassed to crawl into their bed, so I would stand hovering over my sleeping mother until she sensed my presence and made room for me. This almost always managed to startle her. "You scared the crap out of me," she'd say groggily as she scooted over. Like I said earlier, anything can be frightening if it appears out of nowhere in the dark. Including me, in an old-fashioned nightgown. I must have looked like a child ghost who had just floated in from the nineteenth century.

As soon as I felt my mother near me, I was at peace and fell right to sleep. But this did not curb the humiliation I felt at the casual mention of my problem. I remember being eight years old and sitting around the dinner table on Christmas night, and my dad telling my Aunt Deloris how tired he was. "We were up all night setting up the presents and then Lizzie came into the bed . . ." *No!* I thought to myself, *please, don't tell anyone my secret!*

"She's still crawling into your bed?" Aunt Deloris asked, surprised. *Still? This is something you've mentioned before, Dad? Just how many people know about this?* He didn't mean to embarrass me, but I felt mortified at any mention of my co-dependent sleep problem.

My biggest worry was that it would never get better. That I would be twenty years old, crawling into bed with my mom, the subject of tabloid fodder. *College Girl Too Scared to Sleep Alone!* the headline would read. I knew things needed to change.

As the years went on, slowly, my nightly episodes became weekly episodes, and then monthly, and slowly tapered off from there. By the time I started high school, I had almost completely stopped going into my parents' room.*

You would think that for someone like me, leaving home for college would have been a frightening proposition. Quite the contrary; not only was I excited for all the exciting things college life in Southern California had to offer, I was excited to finally have a roommate. At long last, I would have someone to share a room with. I was convinced that just having someone else in the room would help me fall asleep faster and sleep more solidly. I was right. I even became friends, and eventually roommates, with a girl, Yasmina, who had a similar history of sleep issues. We would laugh as we compared stories of our fathers sneaking out of our rooms. Her father, a distinguished Chicago judge, would be reduced to crawling out of the room on all fours. "My poor dad had to commando out of the room," she would say, and the image always got a good laugh out of me.

After college I shared an apartment with a couple of fellow Loyola students. Brian and I had been really good friends in school, and Linda and I were just getting to know each other. The more Linda and I talked, the more we found we had in

---

* Save for a few isolated episodes when I was *really* scared.

common. When the subject of sleep came up, we found that we had the exact same neuroses. She even heard the soldiers in her pillow! What were the chances? America truly is an amazing melting pot.

Linda and I became very close—so close, in fact, that I was not ashamed to sprint to her room and leap into bed with her on nights when we had viewed a horror movie and my old demons came back to haunt me. Linda is very attractive, so my guy friends love to fixate on the thought of the two of us in bed, as though there were some hot lesbian action taking place. The reality was far less sexy, but way more entertaining. Two overimaginative girls in their early twenties, scared shitless as they tried to figure out what the crunching outside the window could be. One time a flashlight darted through the window, and Linda swiftly, and with brute force, rolled me away from the window, out of harm's way, whispering "Don't move" with the authority of a platoon sergeant. Turns out it was just our call-girl neighbor looking for her lost puppy.

After I married Pat, my sleep was the most solid of my life. Finally, someone was contractually obligated to sleep next to me every night. On nights when he was out of town, I would turn on every light and television in the house and stay awake until dawn,* but it was a small price to pay for the security of the rest of our nights together.

All of this history is merely a preamble to my inability to teach my children to be independent sleepers. My son, Michael, has never been a good sleeper; I can't help but feel

---

* When it is "safe" to close your eyes.

that I am mostly to blame for this. Not only has he inherited my bad-sleeper genes, but he has me as his mother, enabling this behavior since babyhood. It didn't completely start out this way; in the beginning I tried to do the right thing.

When Michael was about eight months old, Pat and I decided that we had to do something to end the sleep deprivation that was turning us into such cranky bastards. We were sick of pretending to be happy for other parents who would excitedly tell us how their child "has been sleeping from seven p.m. until seven a.m. since she was nine weeks old!" "That's amazing," we'd say, with fake smiles plastered on our exhausted faces. "That's so great, good for you!"

We knew from parenting books and friends with children that Michael was physically able to sleep for twelve straight hours. We just needed to commit to training him. Some kids are naturally good sleepers, and others have to be trained.

There is an entire enterprise dedicated to training babies to sleep. The term *sleep training* sounds like something out of a science fiction movie to me. I imagined babies lined up on cots, suction cups attached to their heads, while German ladies with clipboards monitored oversized computers, barking out orders to any baby who awoke. I actually would have preferred this. What sleep training actually involved was much worse, as far as I was concerned. It basically boiled down to letting your child cry so that he learns to comfort himself and fall asleep on his own.

There are lots of different ways to go about this. Some methods involved a lot of crying and no intervention, and others permitted you to enter the room after an allotted amount of time and give the baby verbal reassurance, such as, "It's okay, you're doing great. We love you. It's bedtime." But all of the methods appeared to have the same result, which was, after three nights of hell, your kid would sleep through the night on his own.

I opted for the method that included the verbal reassurance, even though the idea of speaking sweetly to a weeping child as if all is well, while refusing to touch him, creeped me out and went against every mothering instinct I had. But I knew that I had to do something, and all the experts claimed that it was not harmful. I chose to believe the experts, and Pat and I went for it.

The first couple of nights were traumatic for me. Pat had to physically restrain me from going into Michael's room to comfort him. These confrontations were often overly dramatic, like something you'd see in a made-for-TV movie about drug abuse or eating disorders or anything more serious than getting a baby to sleep. Pat would shake me by the shoulders and stare into my eyes desperately. "You cannot go in there! We've got to stick to the plan, Lizzie. We've come this far; we can't turn back now. We're so close!"

At first, the plan was a success. After the magical third night, Michael would go to sleep on his own and comfort himself back to sleep. But then, after a couple of months, things started to unravel. Michael was cutting some more teeth and waking often. The women on the *Sleepy World* CD that I had purchased had been very specific that if your child is teething or sick, you should not let him cry. That was all I needed to hear. I reverted to comforting him in the middle of the night, usually through breastfeeding. After his teeth came through, we had to go back to square one, and this time it was much more challenging.

The way the training is structured, you go in with your verbal reassurance after ten minutes, and then the next time fifteen minutes, and then twenty-five, and so on. One time we were visiting my parents in Las Vegas, and Michael had been crying for almost half an hour. My mom wondered why I wasn't going into the room. I explained about the sleep training and how one time I had to let him cry for forty-five minutes. My mom had a look on her face like she had just discovered I was a hired assassin. "Forty-five minutes?" she asked, unsure if she had understood me correctly.

"Yeah. Didn't you do that with us?" I asked, desperate for reassurance.

"No, never." Seeing the tears form in my eyes and sensing that I was about to melt down, she added, "But maybe we should have; you're probably doing the right thing, honey."

"Oh my God, I'm a monster!" I went running into the room where Michael was sleeping, picked him up, and never let him cry again.

Now I have a toddler who won't go to sleep unless Daddy or Mommy lies down with him, and he wakes up in the middle of the night needing one of us to come back into his room. The process of putting him to bed can take up to an hour on some nights. Just when you think he is down and try to slip out, he rolls over and grabs your arm, saying, "Cozy me."

I am certain that this is my penance for the years of bedtime hell I put my parents through. One time I had the nerve to complain to my mother about Michael's bedtime problem. At first she was sympathetic, but then she couldn't hold it in any longer. She started laughing and could not stop. "It's coming back to haunt you! I can't wait to hang up and tell Daddy!"

Much as I deserve this, I feel terrible that my husband has to pay the price for my sins. There is not a lot I can do at this point. I am completely ill-equipped to remedy this situation. I can't help but empathize with my son. No one knows the terror of having to sleep alone like I do. How can I be tough with him about his sleep issues when my own have never been solved? I am too guilt-ridden to leave the room, and when I do, it is often on all fours.

How can you calm someone's fear when you yourself are terrified? Kids have crazy imaginations, but so do I. So when my son tells me in the dark, "There's a guy over there, Mommy!" it scares the shit out of me. I want to say, "Where? What does he look like?!" And when he tells me that he doesn't know, I want to yell, "Well, it's either a ghost or the bogeyman, Michael! We need to figure this out! Was he wearing a top hat?" But instead, I rub his head tenderly and tell him there's nothing to be afraid of, as my eyes dart around the room nervously, making sure there is no sign of a witch, a demon, or the Incredible Hulk.

Discussion Questions

1. Has Elizabeth's guilt made things worse for her son? Do you think Michael will be doomed to a life of co-dependent sleep because his mother feels too terrible to ignore his cries in the night?

2. Which things that you feel guilty about will help you

impose guilt on your children? Which things that you feel guilty about will do more harm than good?

Summary

The Guilt and Manipulation philosophy (or worldview, as I am likely to call it when I am feeling particularly high and mighty about my own bullshit) is, by its nature, dependent on a deep-rooted understanding of the nature of guilt. Not just an academic understanding, but also an understanding based on life experience. Because of this, it is unavoidable that you will feel terrible about yourself as a parent from time to time. This is natural, and without it, these methods would be shallow and phony. Embrace your guilt, but be careful that your own feelings of guilt do not cripple your efforts to raise well-adjusted children.

Oh crap. I thought I was done, but this letter just came flying at my front door. That's weird; I thought the mail already came today.

Dear Elizabeth,

I was forced to read your book for my marriage and family class. Are you kidding me? I had to sit through your pathetic, pointless rambling about wanting your neighbors to think you're hot. What does that have to do with anything? Give me a break, lady. By the way, I know it was you who called the police and broke up our party two weeks ago.

Signed,
One of the guys next door

P.S. I do not think you are hot. Between your glasses and that stupid hat you wear when you walk your dog, I spent my first couple of weeks here thinking I lived next door to Woody Allen.

Probably for the best if I don't respond to this one. I'm going to close my blinds now.

Grandma Guido* and the Evolution of Guilt and Manipulation

"Wear two pairs of pantyhose and keep your knees together!"

—*Dating advice from Grandma Guido*

"You'd better start praying to the Blessed Mother for forgiveness!" *"When I'm dead you'll be sorry you didn't eat this sfingi."*† *"Why don't you want to spend time with your grandmother? When I'm gone you'll wish you had taken me to bingo!"*

If any of these statements have the ring of familiarity to you, then either you are a relative of mine, or you grew up

---

* Pronounced *Guy-dough*, as opposed to the more common *Gwee-dough*. Although it should be noted that certain relatives prefer the latter pronunciation and use it with a great deal of pride.

† An Italian doughnut deep-fried in olive oil, which in the eyes of some relatives renders it a "healthy" alternative to a regular doughnut.

with a grandmother or mother who implemented this style of take-no-prisoners guilt distribution.

Before we go any further, our legal department would like us to make the following statement:

The Guilt and Manipulation Institute does not endorse Grandma Guido's method of guilt and manipulation. We present the methods of Grandma Guido for scientific purposes only, in an effort to understand the evolutionary elements of guilt. If you are tempted to use any of her tactics or catchphrases, it should be done cautiously and only after you have acquired a certain level of experience (or if you are one of the few naturally gifted ones born with the sensibility of an eighty-five-year-old Sicilian woman from Brooklyn; if you believe you may fall into this category, please meet with one of our scientists for an interview, examination, and necessary blood work). Gram's method is a powerful one and should be used sparingly.

Familial guilt is something that evolves from generation to generation. Without even being aware of it, we have adapted the psychological tactics of our forebears, morphing them to suit our personalities and the time and place we are living in. After careful examination, it has become clear that my mother's technique of sly, furtive guilt is a direct descendant of my grandmother's overt, in-your-face guilt.

Our style of parenting is determined not only through genetics, but by a multitude of variables, including nature, nurture, and the hand we have been dealt. Let us look at how this relates by examining my own lineage.

The first time that I consciously experienced guilt was with my Grandma Guido. I was about six years old, and Gram was visiting us for Christmas. I was feeling especially jolly, decorating the tree and munching on a cookie. Crumbs were spilling all over the floor, and Gram barked at me, "Sweep up those crumbs and get a napkin, Elizabeth Ann. Your beautiful mother works hard to keep this house nice; don't let it go to pot!" Later that night I recounted the story to my mother, and in my little voice I said, "She just made me feel so, so . . . *guilty*." It was the first time I used the word. My mother just smiled.

In the scientific community my maternal grandmother's type of personality is commonly referred to as a *chops buster.*[*] Certainly many of my grandmother's traits were genetically predetermined; she entered the world as a buster of chops. But the fact that she was widowed at a young age exasperated this condition, as she was forced to play the dual role of mother and father while raising her four young children. Thus she was a strict disciplinarian who ran a tight ship.

When it came to the distribution of guilt, like many members of her generation, my grandmother used a direct method. Gram would speak her rules clearly and in great detail. She would tell you straight out that you should be ashamed of yourself for defying her: "What a disgrace!" Gram made it clear that by defying her you were also defying Jesus, the Virgin Mary, the Roman Catholic Church, and every dead relative who came before you. A tangible punishment would

---

[*] One who busts chops; aka *ball buster.*

then follow, unlike in our home, where our punishment was the internal pain of having disappointed our parents. There was nothing subtle about Gram or her punishments.

It should be noted that although my grandmother was very strict and an expert at wielding her magical guilt wand, everything she did was out of love, designed to protect you from the evils of this world and save you from eternal damnation. If she thought you were really in trouble, or if you were really sick, Gram would stay up all night praying the rosary for you. No one prayed harder or lit more candles than my Grandma Guido.

You could tell how concerned Grandma was about you by the number of candles she had lit for you at any given time. If she said, "I'll light a candle for you, sweetheart," it meant that she was going to use the power of prayer to help you with whatever you were trying to accomplish; Gram wanted your dreams to come true and she was going to use all of her holy connections to help make it happen. If, however, she said in a threatening manner, "Jesus, Mary, and Joseph . . . I'm lighting a candle for you!" it meant that she was legitimately concerned about the fate of you and your soul. Gram was like a Catholic superhero, but instead of an invisible airplane or webs that shot out of her wrists, Gram had rosary beads and a bottle of holy water clutched in one hand and a change purse full of dollar bills ready to put in the candle vigil donation box in the other. The world was a safer place when she was alive; I miss her dearly and can only imagine that she has been given some kind of important job in the afterlife. When St. Peter retires from working the pearly gates, he will no doubt be replaced by my grandmother, who will quickly gain a reputation for being much tougher to get past.

Grandma Guido was the type of person who would lift you up when you were at your weakest. Schizophrenics were treated like kings, but if you were too successful or too good looking, she'd take you down a few notches: "Look at the aristocrat over here," or, "You've got a face only a mother could love." She did not say these things to bring you down or hurt you, but rather to protect you by keeping the evil eye away. My grandmother and her siblings believed that saying positive things about a person blessed with exceptional beauty or talent could result in an envious person cursing them with the evil eye (or "overlooking" them), resulting in a terrible fate. Although she was Italian Catholic, she was fond of using the Yiddish term *kinehora* when speaking of good things that were happening in the family. She had picked up this evil-eye-deflecting phrase from some of her Jewish friends in her neighborhood and used it in conjunction with her own phrase, "Make the horns, sweetheart," whose origins I'm not entirely sure of, but I get the gist of it.

No one rooted for your success more than Gram, and she would brag about you, in your absence, to *other* people, but to your face she was your harshest critic because she wanted you to succeed and strive for more. My cousin Sebby used to make fun of me because my grandmother would brag about how beautiful she thought I was, saying things like, "Elizabeth Ann looks like a cover girl." But to me she would say, "That hairstyle does nothing for you."

My hair was a source of contention with my grandma. My hair is very wavy and unusually thick, and though hairstylists go crazy for it, it has always been difficult for me to tame. On a good day it is pretty but unruly, very *A Midsummer's Night Dream*; on a bad day, it is more *A Midsummer's Nightmare* starring Roseanne Roseannadanna. When I was away at college, at the height of the O. J. Simpson trial, she sent me a letter encouraging me to get my hair styled like the prosecuting attorney, Marcia Clark, complete with magazine clippings of some of her other "suggestions."

The note and clippings were included in her Halloween card to me. It was a cute little card with an adorable black cat on the front. The cover read, "Just a little note . . ." and the inside continued, ". . . to say 'hi—Happy Halloween!'" At first glance the whole thing appeared sweet and innocent. Then I read the enclosed note:

> *Elizabeth,*
>
> *Are you thinking of a hairstyle change? Enclosed are some of my suggestions. Of course my #1 suggestion is the D.A. (District Attorney). Not pictured. Please heed my suggestions and please—let's get back to normal. You would wow them with the D.A. hairstyle. Hope to see you in the near future.*
>
> *Grandma xx oo xx*

The "let's get back to normal" comment made it seem as if I had a purple Mohawk or some other counterculture hairdo, when in reality I just had regular curly brown hair that apparently my grandmother thought looked terrible on me. The enclosed suggestions consisted of three magazine clippings: a blonde with wispy hair, a redhead with wispy hair, and a porcelain angel doll holding a harp. The doll was blond, but the style was tight and curly, not unlike the district attorney whose hairdo my grandmother coveted. None of the hairstyles looked like anything that would be possible to recreate with my thick, dark locks.

Gram must have really loved Marcia Clark's hair in order for her to see past the fact that she was prosecuting O. J. Gram was a ruthless defender of O. J. Simpson, and we had some of our worst arguments during the O. J. Simpson murder trial. Gram was shamelessly rooting for O. J., and it made my blood boil. She never said that she thought O. J. was innocent, but she would argue passionately in favor of him. I think there were some clear messages that she was trying to send me, and she was using the O. J. trial as a conduit. She would say things like, "That woman was out drinking those margaritas, like some kind of floozy!"

I would shout back, appalled, "So she deserved to die?"

"Did you see those pictures of her with the margaritas, three sheets to the wind? Disgraceful!"

I thought of the many photos of myself, posed with beverages that I was not legally permitted to drink at the time, and I could feel my face get hot with shame. My grandmother might as well have been stabbing me with the cannoli she was trying to force me to eat.

My cousin Jim's theory was that O. J.'s victory was symbolic for my grandmother. When she was a little girl in New York, her immigrant father, an innocent man, was shot and killed by a policeman, in what could only be explained as a case of mistaken identity. The whole thing was swept under the rug, the cop was never punished, and she never learned all of the details. Grandma felt a kinship with African Americans who had been unfairly prosecuted, and to live to see a black man get away with murder was proof that times had changed.

Maybe. Although getting in a couple of zingers indicating that it is better to be dead than perceived as a drunken floozy was probably on her mind as well. I hate to think it, but it seemed that O. J. being found not guilty validated Gram's deeply entrenched Old World belief that sexually repressed women go to Heaven, while women who drink margaritas with men who aren't their husbands get what's coming to them.

Now that you have a better idea of Gram's personality, let us examine the differences between her style of guilt versus that of her oldest child, my mother. We'll begin with a typical parenting issue and study the different way my grandmother and mother approached it.

Curfews: Gram Vs. Mom	
Gram—Enforced a strict 11:00 p.m. curfew. Yelled at you just as hard if you showed up at 11:01 p.m. or 4:00 a.m. One time locked her son out of the house for defying curfew, making him spend the night in the hallway. But, not wanting him to be cold, threw a blanket on him. Would say in plain language, "If you love your mother, you'll come home on time."	**Mom**—Did not enforce a curfew at all. Rather, told us to call her if we were going to be out past midnight. Her reasoning? Did not want us to rush home in an attempt to meet curfew and get into a car crash and die. Also, believed in the reverse psychology of not having to be home at a certain time. Believed that, if given freedom, her children would come home at a decent hour to prove how responsible they were.

Although studying punishment, or lack thereof, is important, the more revealing thing to look at is what comes after: forgiveness. Let us take a moment to examine the custom of forgiveness and the different ways it was practiced by my grandmother and mother.

For Grandma Guido, the act of forgiveness and the pageantry surrounding it was one of the greatest tools in her toolbox of psychological torment. Gram would forgive you, but that didn't mean she would accept your apology. Believe me, there is a difference. Gram would make you beg for her forgiveness, killing you with her silence. I can think of countless occasions in which, guilt-ridden after one of our arguments, I would approach her with an apology. Gram wouldn't even look up from her crossword puzzle. One hand held her pencil while the other stirred her cup of Postum, the spoon hitting the inside of her cup repetitively. Clank. Clank. Clank. After a while the sound was like Chinese water torture. It was the sound of her not acknowledging you. It was the sound of the final nail in the coffin as Gram took her victory lap by reducing you to a flustered, groveling idiot who didn't even deserve the dignity of a response.

Grandma Guido would win every time with this approach. She succeeded in making you apologize while making you feel even worse about yourself. This would in turn make you feel angry and resentful, which would eventually lead to feeling even guiltier than you had before you approached her with the apology. Gram had the ability to send her children and grandchildren into a guilt death spiral that was difficult for even the strongest of us to recover from.

My mother's approach to forgiveness was different from

that of her mother, Grandma Guido. My mom would forgive you immediately, but in a neutral manner devoid of sugar. She let you know right away that she had forgiven you, but it was clear through her tone that you had better not make the same mistake again. On many occasions, drowning in guilt, I would apologize over and over to my mom, and she would say, "Stop saying you're sorry; just say that you won't do it again." In other words, an apology is just a bunch of meaningless words unless you are willing to correct your behavior. This has stuck with me throughout the years. Well done, Mom.

Though she loved and respected her mother, my mom decided early on that she would bring her own children up very differently. The way my mom saw it, there was no point in hounding your kids for every little thing they did wrong. At a certain point, reasoned my mother, your kids would stop caring if they screwed up, since every mistake was greeted with the same amount of obvious disappointment. Why bother coming home on time if you're still going to get yelled at for going out at all? You can see where she was going with this, right? My mother's conscious choice to do things differently, combined with the inescapable cultural guilt, fused together and formed the (perhaps unintentional) parenting style that I have attempted to deconstruct and present to you in this tome.

It is undeniable that my grandmother's approach to guilt was more blatant and intentional than that of my parents, but on close examination, following a series of interviews, the Guilt and Manipulation Institute has discovered that Grandma Guido had one or two subtle tricks up her sleeve. These isolated incidents provide a window into the evolutionary process that would yield the sly style of guilt distributed by my mother.

My grandmother's house was the central location for teenaged get-togethers when my mother and her siblings were young. My grandmother would roll up the rug so the kids could dance, and she put out food and soft drinks for everyone. Today, this might be seen as a desperate attempt to be seen as a "cool" parent. It is difficult to imagine that this could have been Grandma Guido's M.O. In fact, she most likely would have been revolted by the idea. As a rule, my grandma would much rather be feared than have a bunch of teenyboppers think she could "relate" to them. No, my grandmother rolled up the rug and had everyone over for one reason only; so she could keep an eye on her kids. If they were going to have fun, it would be under her watchful gaze. This way, if anyone stepped over the line, she would be right there to shoot disapproving daggers their way. It is in methods such as this where we see the seeds of my mother's more covert guilt.

Grandma used guilt on her children and grandchildren very differently from the stealth way in which my parents manipulated us (so stealthily, in fact, that it is doubtful that even they realized exactly what they were doing, which for me is the most impressive part). The great minds at the Guilt and Manipulation Institute Think Tank believe that without my grandmother's straightforward style of guilt distribution, my mother's version would not exist in its current form. There is an evolutionary component to the way guilt and manipulation are interpreted by each generation.

Gram's Advice

Like many grandmothers, Grandma Guido liked to impart the wisdom of her years upon you. One time when I was in my early twenties and was home visiting for Christmas, my grandma gave me some advice. It is important to note that I was on a bit of a high professionally; I had just gotten a big talent deal with ABC, and a few months prior I had been featured in a *Time* magazine article about the future of comedy. For a rare moment, I was feeling pretty good about myself. "Elizabeth Ann," she began, "listen to your Grandmother. I think you should take tap dancing lessons." I was thinking to myself, *Ahh, that's so sweet. Ridiculous, but sweet. Gram probably wants me to be a triple threat, actress/comic/ tap dancer.* Then she proceeded to tap me on the ass and say, "Help get this down a little." The woman who, if she could have, would have hooked me up to an IV of olive oil during my "I eat no fats" college days was now telling me my ass was too big for Hollywood. I could only hope that she was merely attempting to keep the evil eye from affixing my ass with a horrendous curse.

UP CLOSE AND PERSONAL
A Tale of Two Cities— Life With Grandma Guido

My grandmother was a New Yorker through and through. She loved the city and took tremendous pride in the island that had welcomed her parents from Italy as teenagers. She was a first-generation Italian American, and though she was proud of her heritage, my grandmother considered herself an American first, specifically a New Yorker. She had moved from Manhattan to Brooklyn when she was raising her children, and as her kids grew, the farthest any of them went was to Long Island.

So, in 1967, when my mom and dad left Brooklyn to move to Las Vegas, my grandmother felt angry and betrayed. My mom waited until the last possible moment to tell her that they were moving across the country. My mother knew she would get hell for it, so she figured it was better to postpone the inevitable than to suffer unnecessarily.

My mom's instincts proved correct. In the couple of weeks that they had left in Brooklyn, my grandmother gave my parents the cold shoulder, refusing to talk to them unless they came crawling to her, and even then, she was icy. Even if she came over to see the kids (my brothers Frank and Jim, who were very small at the time), she would completely ignore my parents and interact only with the boys. She accused my father of stealing her daughter and grandkids away from her, like he was some kind of lowlife kidnapper. "You're taking her to Las Vegas to live with those crooks!" my grandmother shouted, a reference to my dad's brother-in-law, a professional gambler and unsavory character who had moved to Vegas with my dad's sister, Doris,* and their kids.

Many years later, when my brother Frank was living with Grandma during grad school at Fordham, she had a wooden carving of the skyline of Las Vegas in her Brooklyn apartment. She told my brother, "You see that over there? It's to remind me of when your father took your mother away from me!"

---

* A beloved woman who shared zero characteristics with her frightening husband. I would hate myself if I didn't make a note of this.

It was only after they had already been living in Vegas for a short while, and my mother told Gram she was pregnant again, that tensions started to lift. Gram came out to visit when my brother Patrick was born, and she began visiting for every special occasion thereafter: baptisms, births, first communions, confirmations, graduations, and so on.

When my grandma came to visit, she would bring two pieces of luggage. One suitcase was for her clothing and toiletries, and another one was for food. An entire piece of luggage was dedicated to smuggling pizza and Drake's Cakes from the borough of Brooklyn. I would spot her luggage coming down the conveyor belt at the airport like a sniper perched on a rooftop. You could always tell which bags were my grandma's because she would tie an odd-colored ribbon around the handle, like moss green or burnt orange. She had a blue suitcase and a green suitcase; it was the green one that contained the pirate's treasure of Ring Dings, Yodels, and Devil Dogs. We had only Hostess pastries and a couple of other regional brands in our grocery stores. Drake's Cakes seemed so exotic and exciting in comparison. I romanticized about bringing my lunch to school the next day, imagining myself pretending to be casual as I revealed my prepackaged dessert to everyone at my table. "What's that?" they would ask, awestruck.

"Oh, this?" I would reply. "It's called a Yankee Doodle. It's from New York." I would push the plastic wrapper aside and bite into the preservative-laden chocolate treat, convinced that I was more sophisticated than the peons eating Zingers at the next table. *Dolly Madison? How pedestrian!*

I became obsessed with New York and was almost as bitter

about my parents' move as my grandma was. This bonded my grandmother and me. She encouraged my thirst for all that was New York, teaching me the New York Mets fight song and buying me my very own Statue of Liberty crown and torch. I would march around the house with my torch in the air, my crown slightly askew, singing:

Meet the Mets, meet the Mets,
Step right up and greet the Mets.
Bring your kiddies, bring your wife,
Guaranteed to have the time of your life . . .

I would gripe to my parents, "Why did you guys move from New York? I want to be a New Yorker!" This made my grandmother smile from ear to ear. Almost as big a smile as when I announced that I wanted to change my last name from Beckwith to Beckabella, so that people would know that I was Italian. My poor father.

"When you grow up, you can come live in New York. You can live with Grandma!" she would say in front of my mother, satisfied.

As many trips as Gram made to visit us, we made many pilgrimages to New York as well. Sometimes it would be the whole family; sometimes it would be just one or a couple of us kids going to spend a few weeks in the summer with Gram. When my brother Patrick, who was eleven years old at the time, left to spend most of July with Grandma, he was a skinny little kid who couldn't gain weight if he tried. When he came back, he was fat. No one recognized him when he got off the plane in an entirely new wardrobe, as the clothes he left with no longer fit him. The story of Patrick became a cautionary tale of what could happen if you accepted food every time an Italian relative offered it to you.

By the time I made my first solo trip to visit Gram, I was completely paranoid that I would "pull a Patrick" and return to Las Vegas a fat-ass. My brothers would tease me about the possibility; I would receive cards in the mail from them that said things like, "Have a great time! Don't get fat!" It had been five years since Patrick's legendary trip, and he was now svelte enough to feel good about taunting me.

I couldn't have been more than nine years old at the time. I have a clear memory of staring at a platter of Italian cookies on my Gram's dining room table and for the first time in my life feeling like I shouldn't eat any. My desire to shovel all of the marzipan rainbow cookies into my mouth was dwarfed by the image of my brother Patrick, in his Hefty-sized powder-blue pants, waddling off the airplane. I resigned myself to start being careful about how much and what I consumed during my stay in New York. Which led to my first real battles with my grandmother.

Before my decision to start eating more carefully, my grandma and I were partners in crime. Every night at 11:30 we would have a "midnight snack" and watch Johnny Carson together. Her midnight snack was usually a root beer float. I opted for saltier fare, like dried salami and cheese. Her television was in the dining room of her 1920s duplex, which made our ritual all the more convenient. We would sit at the dining room table, my hair would be drying in the old-fashioned rag-curls she would set it with, and Gram would be in curlers. We would stuff our faces and laugh at Johnny's jokes.

Now when I refused food, Gram would tell me that it was a sin. There were children starving all over the world who would love to eat this food, and it was a sin to waste it. I would argue that regardless of whether I ate the food or didn't eat the food, the starving children would still not have access to it, and then I would add, "Gluttony is a sin, too, Grandma!"

"You'd better just pray to the Blessed Mother for forgiveness!" she would say, huffing off to drink her root beer float alone, which I had now taken all of the pleasure out of.

Suddenly Gram became tougher on me about everything. In the past she would usually let me sleep in while she attended the daily 7:30 a.m. mass alone. Now she would wake me up to go with her.

"It's Tuesday! Why do we need to go to church? I just went on Sunday," I'd say, putting the pillow over my head.

"There are different readings on weekdays. We need to thank the Lord for all of our blessings."

"Let me sleep, and then, on Sunday, I'll thank the Lord for you letting me sleep!"

"I wish my sweet grandmother were alive to take me to daily mass! When I'm dead, you'll wish you had cooperated with your grandmother!"

Though she had taken to riding me about every little thing now that I wasn't eating as much, Gram was still an amazing hostess. Every day was filled with adventure. Of course, she took me to all of the important tourist attractions: the Empire State Building, the World Trade Center, the New York Stock Exchange, the Staten Island Ferry, St. Patrick's Cathedral.

The list goes on and on. Although I soaked up all that New York had to offer, the things that had the biggest impact on me were not the typical vacation stops: walking past the cemetery on the way from the subway to Gram's house, the endless visits to the relatives that I didn't even know I had, the stops at Carvel on the way home from Rockaway Beach. It was on these outings that I learned the most. It was during these trips that Gram taught me to tuck in my gold necklace when I rode the subway and showed me the best way to wear a purse to avoid getting mugged. It was these things that gave me a real sense of what it meant to call New York home.

When I returned to Las Vegas I hadn't gained any weight, but I had gained an accent. Suddenly I was peppering my conversations with the word *yo* and was ending questions with the word *no*. As in, "Yo, Patrick, you're going to the movies tonight, no?"* My grandmother prided herself on her proper command of the English language and did not speak this way, but I had picked up these affectations from various other relatives.

I made many more trips with my family to visit Gram in the years that followed. But in May 1997, I went to her house for the last time. I was twenty-two years old and had joined my parents and Aunt Jenny on a trip to help my grandma move out of the home where she had lived for the last forty-eight years. Her sister, who owned the duplex and had lived on the first floor, had passed away a year earlier, and her sons had other plans with the building.

---

* Eventually I dropped the *yo* and *no* from my conversations, much to the relief of my family. The weird accent I have now, I believe, is independent of my New York experience.

At this point, rent in New York had skyrocketed, and there didn't seem to be anywhere safe that my Gram could afford to live. After brainstorming many different scenarios, it was decided that the best alternative was for my grandmother to move to Las Vegas and live with my parents.

Packing up all of my grandmother's things proved both physically and emotionally draining for everyone. Not surprisingly, my grandmother seemed the least affected by it. But that was just her way, always the tough one. She had made her decision and she wasn't going to look back.

One of my jobs was to clean out a cabinet that housed forty-eight years' worth of every greeting card she had ever received. It was fun strolling down memory lane and reading the messages from all of her kids, grandkids, and great-grandkids throughout the years. What was the most striking was how most of the greeting cards were so wrong for my grandma's personality. It wasn't the fault of the people who sent her the cards; it was the fault of the card companies. All Grandma cards have a variation of the same sentiment: *Grandma, for your warm, gentle touch and all the sweet things you do to make me feel special, Happy Birthday!* Usually this sentiment is accompanied by a cartoonish image of a grandma taking a pie out of the oven, surrounded by chirping birds. Not that my grandmother didn't make me feel special in her own way, it's just that fresh-baked pie wasn't the first thing that popped into my mind when I thought of her. Where were the greeting cards for women like my grandma? Where were the cards that read, *Grandma, for all the candles you lit for me in church when you thought that I had a drinking problem. God bless you on your special day!* Or, *Grandma, for all the times you chased me around the house with a cannoli the size of a football and told me that if I didn't eat it, the Blessed Mother would weep. Happy Birthday!*

Thirty years after my parents made their journey west, my grandmother joined them. It was not an easy transition for someone with such deep roots in New York. My grandmother was leaving behind a lot of friends and relatives and a great many organizations that she was active in. Plus, she was leaving behind her independent lifestyle. Once she moved to Vegas, she would become completely dependent on my parents for transportation. Nonetheless, she was ready to make the move. "I'm going where the people love me," she'd say, in a dig toward the nephews whom she perceived to be kicking her out.

Now that she was sharing a home with them, my parents took my grandma just about everywhere they went. If my parents went on out to dinner, Gram came, too. If my parents went on vacation, Gram came, too. Although my father was seventeen years younger than my grandma, they both had white hair, so they were often mistaken for a couple. This drove my dad nuts. It didn't help that my grandmother would bark out comments like, "Chivalry is dead!" if he was too slow in opening a door for her.

My grandmother, a die-hard Democrat, and my father, a convert to conservatism since Reagan, would have loud arguments about politics. I wish I had videotaped some of these debates; they were far more entertaining than anything the professional pundits on cable news could offer. "Look at these thieves, they're stealing the election! What a disgrace!"

"Boy oh boy, you're never gonna stop with that one.

They're not stealing anything, Ma! They did a recount and Bush won, *fair* and *square*."

"Yeah, and I've got a bridge in Brooklyn to sell you! You worry about the Democrats making this country communist; meanwhile these Republican morons are taking away our votes, and don't you forget it! It's a sin!"

Though she enjoyed busting his chops and pushing his political buttons, Gram loved and respected my dad. This was evident in the way she defended him if anyone, including me, said anything vaguely antagonistic toward him. One time when my dad had cooked up a batch of pancakes, I made an innocent comment that one of mine was a little raw in the middle. "You shouldn't say such things, Elizabeth Ann! Words hurt. They hurt right here," Gram said, pounding her heart.

"I'm just letting him know it needs to go back on for a minute, Gram, geez," I said.

"You might as well be beating him with a stick!" Gram shouted.

Even though she would ride my mother about certain things, like the television shows she enjoyed ("You gotta watch your tripe!") or her posture ("Put your shoulders back! I should have given you dancing lessons; you wouldn't have that hump!"), it was clear how much she loved her and how proud she made her. Whenever I came to visit, Gram would tell me a hundred times how hard my mother worked. "She works so hard, your beautiful mother!" "She's a saint, your mother. A saint!" "When they made your mother they broke the mold!" It was my grandmother who encouraged my mom to hire a cleaning lady when Gram was no longer physically able to help my parents around the house. "You deserve a cleaning lady; you're not a slave!"

By the end of 2001, Gram had started to slow down. It was odd to see my feisty grandmother so slow and tired. Gram had always been busty and broad, and she always looked strong; even well into her seventies she was a better bet to open a difficult jar of pickles than I was. Now, at eighty-eight, she was frail. Suddenly Gram needed help walking down the aisle for communion at mass.

By Mother's Day my grandmother was bedridden. Several days later, they discovered she had cancer. Things deteriorated rapidly after that. I got a call from my mother in the third week of May, and her voice was shaking. My mom has always held it together in front of her children, so I knew by the sound of her voice that something bad was happening. "Grandma's dying," she said. "You should come home."

I drove in from California with my brother Frank and his wife, Frankie (yes, their names are Frank and Frankie). When we arrived at the hospice, they were just bringing a woman in from an ambulance, someone who had been transported from a hospital. The woman was very tiny, and her face was as white as her hair. I remember thinking that she looked like a ghost. "Is that our grandma?" Frank asked.

"No. That's not Gram," I said, confident.

Frank moved closer to get a better look. "It is, Lizzie. That's Grandma."

I didn't really believe that she was dying until that moment. I had always joked that Grandma would outlive us all, and on some level I think I actually believed it. Until those last few months, she was so vibrant and completely had her wits about her. It had been only a few months earlier, at my bridal shower, that she was making me show her that I was wearing a slip and badgering me not to forget the back of my hair. "Don't ignore the back, Elizabeth Ann! It looks like sin!" In spite of her advanced age, this was a woman who seemed like she still had a lot of good years left.

I was there the night Gram died. My mom and her youngest brother, my Uncle Joey, were spending the night at the hospice, and I wanted to be there with them. We were going to take turns sleeping, so that someone would always be awake with Gram; we were discussing who would take the first shift when the night nurse came in to talk to us. She gave us "the talk." It was a variation of a speech that I've since learned many people with dying relatives have been given.

"I wanted to let you know that Frances will probably pass tonight. But she's a fighter, and right now she's fighting it because she thinks you still need her. I've seen this many times. She'll hang on as long as she thinks you're not ready for her to leave. You need to tell her that it's okay to go, and that you'll be okay without her. It is important that you go in one at a time and say good-bye to her and let her know that it's okay to go."

The way the hospice room was set up, there was a little area with a couch and a television, and then there was another room, a bedroom, for the patient. I couldn't help but think of this setup as the living room and the dying room. Following the nurse's advice, we took turns going into the bedroom to have our last words with Gram.

I knew in my heart the nurse was right; it was time to let Grandma go. But part of me still clung to the desperate hope that a miracle would take place. I pictured myself pouring my heart out, telling Gram how much I appreciated her, and how sorry I was to ever have taken her for granted, when suddenly she would bolt upright and say, "I told you you'd be sorry when I was gone! Now do me a favor and fix that mane of yours. Vanity, thy name is woman!" But instead she lay there limp, the time between breaths frighteningly long. I sensed she was listening, though, and I tried my best to make every word count.

My mom went next, and then my Uncle Joey. My uncle had been in there a few minutes when he began calling out, "Nurse! Nurse! I think she's gone, I think she's gone." The nurse had been right. Within seconds of my uncle finishing his good-bye, my grandmother took her last breath.

The next week Pat and I traveled to New York for my grandmother's funeral. The wake and the funeral mass were both packed, and I was happy to see that there were flowers everywhere; it was comforting and it made me proud to see just how popular she really was. My father gave a beautiful eulogy, and he got choked up as he reminisced about their hilarious political bickering. The service was at my Gram's old Brooklyn parish, Blessed Sacrament, the same church whose weekday services Gram had dragged me out of bed for eighteen years earlier. Channeling Gram, I thought to myself, *I wish my sweet grandmother were alive to take me to weekday mass.* My hair came out perfect that day, and somewhere in heaven, Gram was smiling.

Discussion Questions

1. Is Gram's style of guilt and manipulation something that you should sprinkle into your routine, or is it too in-your-face for your personality?
2. Is it more effective to use guilt to get a child to eat, or to use food to make him or her feel guilty about other things?
3. Based on the photo on this book jacket, is Elizabeth's hair in a phase that her grandmother would approve or disapprove of? What style might be more flattering on her?

Summary

Gram's methods are not for everyone and should be used sparingly. They are an interesting topic of study from a scientific perspective; the Guilt and Manipulation philosophy stems from them, as both an evolution of them and a rebellion from them. Experiment with extreme caution and always remember, "The Blessed Mother's watching you!"

Frequently Asked Questions

Did this method originate with your family? How long has the guilt and manipulation method been around?

Although my ancestors had a great handle on this technique, and my parents perfected it, they did not invent this method. The Guilt and Manipulation philosophy has been around for more than two thousand years. Why do you think we never hear much about Jesus' teenaged years? Sure, he was the Son of God, but that's not the only reason he behaved himself. It has been said that all Mary had to do was give Jesus "the look" and he would stop in his tracks. It is rumored that biblical scholars have unearthed a missing book of the Bible, the Book of Mary, which includes such passages as, "What the hell do you mean she rubbed oil on your feet?" and, "I know about your tantrum at the temple, so don't bullshit me."

My child is already twelve years old, and he is a nightmare; is it too late to start this method? Can he be saved?

It is never too late to begin this approach, though it is more challenging if you are beginning during the middle school years, but rest assured, it can be done. You may have to adjust the order of things a bit, beginning with the appearance of freedom and then layering in the guilt before applying the final layers of manipulation. Take it slowly; remember that twelve-year-olds are naturally cynical beings, so mind games are going to be crucial here. Don't be shy; apply mind control techniques liberally and add *Please lead my son down the right path, keeping him happy, healthy, and safe* to your obsessive nightly prayer ritual.*

Can I use these methods on friends and co-workers?

At this point in time, we do not recommend using the Guilt and Manipulation philosophy on people outside your family. The Guilt and Manipulation Institute is currently perform-ing experiments in this arena, but the method has not been approved for the public yet. Stay tuned.

I am a stepparent; is it appropriate for me to use these methods on my stepchild?

Absolutely! You will be doing the child and his biological parents a huge favor. In order for this to be a success, it is

---

* Having an obsessive-compulsive prayer ritual and encouraging your children to have their own neurotic series of prayers is highly recom-mended by the Guilt and Manipulation Institute. For the parent, it pro-vides divine reassurance, while for the children it provides a reminder that God is watching. This is much more effective than the notion that Santa is watching, as Santa can only deprive them of gifts, not sentence them to eternal damnation in a fiery inferno. (I have included my own childhood prayer ritual at the end of this book if your child doesn't know where to begin.)

vital that you gain the child's trust first. Try bonding with the child through activities and interests that he enjoys, and then, once you feel a strong connection, begin commenting. Start with positive comments you know he will agree with to cement your relationship. ("The Baseball Hall of Fame sounds amazing. You know, we should plan a trip to Cooperstown.") Then, when the moment feels right, commence peppering the conversation with comments that will be crucial in shaping his behavior and worldview. ("Is Barry Bonds for real? Of course he did steroids. Who ever heard of a man's foot going from a size ten to a thirteen AFTER AGE *THIRTY-FIVE*?! What a disgrace! If they put him in the Hall of Fame, it better be with an asterisk!") Warning: Do not attempt to use these methods to poison the child's mind about his biological parents. That is unethical and will most likely backfire on you. No matter how big a jerk the kid's mother may be, do not give in to temptation.

Elizabeth, you speak a lot about your Italian family, but your family name is Beckwith, which is very lockjaw British sounding. Explain.

Yes, my mother's side is the Italian side, and as is often the case with people who marry Italians, the Italian side took over and dominated the culture of our home. Although my father's name makes us sound like a troop of Shakespearean thespians, he grew up in Astoria, Queens, and has a very New York personality that blends seamlessly with my mother's side of the family. Additionally, two of my father's siblings also married Italians; thus I had Italian cousins on both sides of my family, so those traditions were a big part of my childhood no matter which side we were spending the holidays with.

Do you have a guilt and manipulation training program for nannies and caregivers?

We are currently fine-tuning the logistics and curriculum for an intensive, two-week-long Guilt and Manipulation Nanny Camp. Our goal is to be able to offer this program by the summer of 2011 (check our Web site for status). Classes and activities will most likely include Snack Attack (food manipulation basics), Facial Yoga (mastering "the look" in five easy moves), and Crash Course Commenting (phrases that you can use right away to get results, beginning with the concrete "Does she look like a hooker or what?" and graduating to the abstract "What the hell is that supposed to mean?").

I am intrigued by the title of your forthcoming book, Elizabeth Learns That Tits Trump a Pretty Face; *would it be too much to ask for an excerpt?*

No problem. Please enjoy the following passage from the introduction:

> *In my sophomore year of college, I spent my Christmas break working as an extra in the film* Casino. *I had been chosen as one of the "beautiful girls" to be seated at a table with Robert De Niro. I was thrilled. I got to go to hair and makeup and wear an amazing retro outfit that actual wardrobe people fitted me for. Best of all, people in the know thought I was*

beautiful! What could be better? While I was waiting to have my hair done, a couple of other girls walked in, holding costumes. I thought they were just moderately attractive; they looked like middle school kids as far as I was concerned. Then they got into their costumes. Oh my God, it was like a giant-titty parade! These girls looked amazing in their outfits; I couldn't believe the transformation. Suddenly my glamorous ensemble felt ridiculous. I looked down at my chest and sadly thought, "Maybe I'm the one who looks like she's in middle school."

The next thing I knew, the assistant director was explaining to me that there had been a change of plans and I would be in a different scene the next day. I would no longer be a "beautiful girl"; I would be "frozen yogurt girl" and wear a big coat and polyester pants. One of my dad's friends, a real old-time Vegas guy, was working as an extra, too. He saw this all go down and jokingly called out, "If you want to be in the movie, you'd better get yourself some tits, kid!" I laughed, pretending to be affable.

Until that point, I had been walking blindly through life thinking that a pretty face was more important than tits. I was wrong.

Thank You and Good Luck

Now that your tutorial is complete, it's time to turn the theoretical into action. As I stated at the beginning of this book, start slowly. Many of these methods require that you ease into them, or you risk coming across as a phony who is merely posturing. Take your time, breathe, and when you get frightened, remember that you are not alone. All over the world parents are turning back the clock, using guilt, shame, and the fear of death to keep their children on the straight and narrow.

You may have noticed throughout this book that I make more than a couple of references to your child respecting you (along the lines of, "If he respects you at all, your child will feel ashamed"). For the Guilt and Manipulation philosophy to work, it is crucial that your children respect you. Respect is something that has to be earned. So before you set out to use the guilt and manipulation approach, make sure you are worthy of this respect. In other words, don't be an asshole.

Thank you, and best of luck as you set out on the highly rewarding journey of guilt-infused parenting.

Recipes to Keep
Your Children from
Running Away

"What do you mean, keep your children from running away? How can a recipe be so powerful?" Have you not been paying attention at all? Get it together! Food is the single greatest environmental control that you have over your family. Use it or lose it! The recipes in this section are designed to help those of you who don't have any traditional family recipes to draw from. What follows are a couple of memorable dishes from my youth, and one very simple, basic dish that I loved as a tiny child (even a complete novice should be able to handle it). Hopefully these will jump-start you as you begin experimenting with food as a means of mind control.

I have always maintained that a healthy, happy family life includes delicious food—food that somehow manages to appear as though you have slaved over it, while at the same time garnering comments like, "You make it look so easy!" In other words, anyone else would die trying to whip this up, but it is just one of your many talents that you share out of love for your family. This establishes a firm foundation of guilt, and then goes a step further by lulling your family into a food coma in which they are easily susceptible to your suggestions.

Bon appetit!

Mom's Sunday Sauce With Meatballs

If you join my family for sauce at my parents' house, it is inevitable that you will spill some on your shirt (unless you dine in the tradition of my Uncle Joe Dimino and create a bib/kerchief out of your napkin). This mark is known in our family as the "red badge of courage." It would be a stretch to say that the stain is worn with pride, but it is sported without the humiliation that typically accompanies one who has sloppily splashed food on himself.

The smell of my mom's sauce cooking all day on the stove is the smell of home. If you come to my parents' house on a Sunday, you can smell it as soon as you get out of your car as you make your way to the front door. It is a signature aroma. If I close my eyes, the smell can transport me to countless moments in time. It is the smell of birthday celebrations, lively political debates, and Easter. If I am not careful, the scent alone can send me into a hypnotic trance, like some kind of captive being drugged by mind control–inducing fumes on an alien craft. Because of the many life lessons absorbed while wolfing them down, these meatballs are in many ways responsible for my worldview.

It should also be noted that although I, at times, took Sunday dinner for granted, many of my friends throughout the years did not. There were countless times when I was finished eating and ready to run and play, but my friends would remain at the table, eating meatballs in a trance. Remember, the longer you can keep your kids and their friends at the table, the less time there is for them to injure themselves or engage in illicit activities (or injure themselves while engaging in illicit activities, for that matter).

Serves: about 6

Sauce:

2 large (28 oz.) cans crushed tomatoes

1 large can water

¼ white onion, finely chopped

½ teaspoon salt

½ teaspoon garlic powder

¼ teaspoon black pepper

⅛ teaspoon crushed red pepper flakes

1 pound hot Italian sausage

1 teaspoon dried oregano

½ cup red wine

2 tablespoons chopped fresh basil

Mix together the sauce ingredients (excluding the wine and basil) in a large pot and bring to a boil. Reduce heat to a simmer. Get to work on your meatballs.

Meatballs:

1 pound chopped sirloin

3 eggs

¼ cup grated Parmigiano-Reggiano

½ cup bread crumbs

1 tablespoon chopped fresh basil (or ½ teaspoon dried basil)

Mix the meatball ingredients with about ¼ cup cold water; you may need to add more water to get the desired moistness. Form into 12–15 balls.

When the sauce has simmered for 15 minutes, add the meatballs. Continue to cook the sauce over low heat until thickened (at least 2 hours). Add the wine 15 minutes before serving and the basil right before serving. Add salt, pepper, and garlic powder to taste.

Serve with your favorite pasta. Be sure to put out a bowl of grated Parmigiano-Reggiano for people to sprinkle on top.

Make sure you are the last one to sit down at the table so your family can get a sense of how hard you worked to prepare this feast.

Dad's French Toast

It seems like only yesterday that I would awaken to the sound of Teflon hitting tile as the aggravated voice of my father rose above the clanging pots: "Son of a bitch! Who put these pans away like this? Dammit to hell!" *Could this mean what I think it means?* I would ask myself, rubbing the sleep from my eyes.

Moments later the scent of nutmeg would waft into my room and my suspicions would be happily confirmed: *French toast!*

My mother is an amazing cook, but my dad gives her a run for her money, particularly with breakfast. My father is such a great breakfast cook that every New Year's morning my parents would host an open house for our relatives and close friends. My father, wearing a chef hat and an apron that read *Goose the Cook*, would fill the banquet-sized chafing dishes with his various culinary delights—one of which was this legendary French toast. Minutes later it would all be gobbled up by hungry relatives, some of whom had arrived an hour before the actual start time of the event. (There are few people in my family who are too ashamed to be first in line at a buffet.)

Serves: 4

4 eggs
4 heaping tablespoons
  powdered sugar
2 splashes milk
2 teaspoons vanilla extract

6 dashes nutmeg
Cinnamon
Cooking oil
8 thick slices white bread or
  "Texas Toast"

Beat the eggs in a bowl. Add the sugar, milk, vanilla, and nutmeg. Beat until the sugar is fully absorbed into the mixture. Dip the bread into the mixture on both sides, lightly perforating it with a fork as you go. Squeeze out any excess liquid as you remove the bread from the mixture. Sprinkle cinnamon lightly but evenly on both sides of the bread. Lay 4 slices of bread in a preheated, oiled rectangular frying pan set over medium heat. Turn over when the bread is browned and cook until the second side is done. Repeat for the remaining slices of bread. Serve with syrup, powdered sugar, or preserves.

Aunt Doris's Eggs on Toast

My dad's sister, Doris, lived with us on and off throughout my childhood. She slept on the couch in our den and took care of me while my parents were at work. Aunt Doris was an insomniac, so she would sleep very late in the morning. Up until she moved in, I thought that only teenaged boys slept past 10:00 a.m. I would hover near the couch and whisper, "Are you almost awake?" In her silky black robe, she would whisper back in a half-dream state, "Five more minutes." I entertained myself by putting her D-cup bras on over my pajamas and pretending to smoke her Salems.

Soon she would rise, and while she sipped her coffee she would make me my "snack." I requested the same snack every day around 11:00. Eggs on toast.

She was so sweet to me; as she handed me my plate, she'd called me "her little tomato" or her "lovin's from the ovens." This makes me feel all the worse for having woken her up all those years ago. I think of her when my kids wake me up before I am ready. If I could do it all over, Aunt Doris, I not only would have let you sleep longer, I would have joined you.

Serves: 1 or 2 hungry children, for breakfast or snack

2 eggs
2 pieces of toast
Butter
Salt

Butter a frying pan. Fry the eggs over medium heat, sunny side up or over easy. Sprinkle with a dash of salt. Serve the cooked eggs on top of buttered toast. Cut into triangle shapes, letting the yolk run all over the toast.
    Lie back down on the couch while the child eats.

Elizabeth's Childhood
OCD Prayer Ritual

BEGIN WITH THE SIGN OF THE CROSS (TWO TIMES).

Our Father, who art in heaven, hallowed be thy name. Thy kingdom come. Thy will be done, on earth as it is in heaven. Give us this day our daily bread, and forgive us our trespasses, as we forgive those who trespass against us. Lead us not into temptation, but deliver us from evil. For thine is the kingdom and the power and the glory, now and forever. Amen.

Hail Mary, full of grace, the Lord is with thee. Blessed art thou amongst women, and blessed is the fruit of thy womb, Jesus. Holy Mary, mother of God, pray for us sinners, now and at the hour of our death. Amen.

Glory be to the Father and to the Son and to the Holy Spirit. As it was in the beginning, is now, and ever shall be, world without end. Amen.

Dear God, please watch over me and protect me and guide me. Keep me happy, healthy, and safe. God bless Mom, Dad, Frank, Jimmy, Patrick, and Rebel. God bless Grandma and all of my aunts, uncles, cousins, and other relatives, and everyone I know, even my enemies. Watch over them, protect them, and guide them. Please keep everyone happy, healthy, and safe, even my enemies (unless of course their safety would result in the pain of others). Please let me fall asleep quickly and without any terrible dreams, unless for some reason it is your will that I have a terrible dream; I don't want to interfere. But I would prefer to not have any terrible dreams, if that is possible; I hope that is your will. But I understand if it isn't. Like I said, I don't want to interfere with your plan.

MAKE THE SIGN OF THE CROSS (TWO TIMES).

*REPEAT **OUR FATHER.***

*REPEAT **HAIL MARY.***

*REPEAT **GLORY BE.***

MAKE THE SIGN OF THE CROSS (FOUR TIMES).

Acknowledgments

There are many people who were generous with their time and talent during the completion of this book. First and foremost, I must thank my parents, Elizabeth and Harold "Pat" Beckwith, for being the inspiration behind this entire concept. They read early excerpts of this and pretended not to be uncomfortable with anything. Thank you.

I would also like to thank:

My husband, Patrick Wuebben, who not only provided valuable feedback, but was the captain of the ship when it came to juggling our family's schedule in order for me to get this finished on time.

My brothers, Francis, James, and Patrick Beckwith, who read early portions of this manuscript and were instrumental in reminding me of disturbing family facts worthy of inclusion.

My in-laws, Jennifer Wuebben Garcia, who spent most of the summer at our house helping me with the children, and Rod Wuebben, who could be counted on to pop over on a moment's notice to lend a hand.

Other people who read early portions of this work and gave me priceless feedback and insights: Bethany Rogers, Yasmina Madden, Brian Liscek, Ann Marie Catricala-McCurdy,

James Sclafani, and my manager, Willie Mercer, who was relentless in making sure this book happened. Also, Bill Zotti and Stuart Manashil at CAA, who have shown endless enthusiasm for this project.

My book agent, Frank Weimann, and his team at the Literary Group (a special shout-out* to Jaimee Garbacik, who helped me refine the original proposal); I appreciate all of your hard work and advice.

My editor, Mary Ellen O'Neill, and her crew at Harper-Collins; thank you so much for championing this project.

Lastly, a big thank-you to the current recipients of my guilt and manipulation: my children, Michael and Frances. I love you so much and I pray to God that you will never read this book (at least not until after you graduate from college).

---

* No, I am not being ironic using the term *shout-out*, although, admittedly, I am a little less comfortable with the phrase than I am with the expression *my peeps*, which I stand behind proudly.